Miss Bellard's Inspiration

A Novel

By W. D. Howells

Author of
"Letters Home" "Questionable Shapes"
"Literary Friends and Acquaintance"
"Literature and Life" etc.

Miss Bellard decides to visit her aunt and uncle in order to consider quietly the questio of marrying a certain eager young Englishman. Clincident with her visit came that of the Mevisions, a couple trembling upon the verge of separation. Thus Muss Bellard is treated to a variety of domestic relations which produced varying effects upon her.

New York and London
Harper & Brothers Publishers
1905

Miss Bellard's Inspiration

Miss Bellard's Inspiration

I

"MY dear, will you please read that letter again?" Mrs. Crombie said, in tones that might either be those of entreaty for her husband's compliance, or command of his obedience, or appeal to his clearer impression from the confusion which her niece's letter had cast her into. She began in a high, imperative note, and ended in something like an imploring whimper. She had first read the letter herself, and then thrown it across the breakfast-table to Crombie; and as he began to read it to himself she now added, "Aloud!"

"I don't see any use in that," he said. "There's no mystery about it."

"No mystery, when a girl like Lillias Bellard starts up out of space and asks a thing like that? We might as well sell the place at once. It will be as bad as The Surges before the summer is over; and I did think that if we came and built inland we could have a little peace of our lives." Crombie trivially thought of saying, "Little pieces of our lives," but he did not, and she went on: "If it's going on like this, the mountains will be as bad as the seashore, and there will be nothing left but Europe. *Give* me that letter, Archibald!"

She recovered it from his wanderingly extended left hand, his right being employed in filling up his cup with the exactly proportioned due of hot milk which he poured so as to make a bead on the surface of the coffee.

"I can't make Lillias out," Mrs. Crombie

this by-gone hollow of the hills, on the wrong side of the Saco, and built a tumble-down old farm-house over so as to be alone in it."

"Then you oughtn't to have built the old farm-house over so nicely. Lillias will go away, and tell everybody that you've got electric lights, and hot and cold water, and a furnace, and all the modern conveniences, and the most delightful rambling camp, with ten or twenty bedrooms, and open fires for cold days in every one. She will say that it isn't dull here a bit; that there's a hotel full of delightful people just across the Saco, which you get to by private ferry, and hops every night, with a young man to every ten girls, and picnics all the time, and lots of easy mountain-climbing."

"Yes, that is the worst of it. Very well, I shall telegraph her not to come, I don't care what happens. I shall say, 'Very sorry. Uncle sick; not dangerously; but all taken up with him.' That's just ten words."

"Twelve; and not one true. Besides, where will you telegraph her? She's started. She left Kansas City yesterday."

"Nonsense!"

"All the same, that's what's happened."

"Very well, then, I know what I shall do. I shall engage a room for her at The Saco Shore, if it's full of such delightful people—"

"Hold on, my dear! That was merely my forecast of her language."

"No matter! And you can meet her at the station and tell her what I've done, and take her there. I am not going to be scooped up, even if she *is* my niece. And so Lillias Bellard will find out."

Mrs. Crombie gathered the offending letter and its envelope violently together, and started from the table as if to go at once and carry out her declared purpose. But she really went up-stairs to decide which of the bedrooms she should give the girl. She began with the worst and ended with the best, which looked eastward in that particular crook of the river towards the Presidential range, and, if you poked your head out, commanded a glimpse of the almost eternal snows of Mount Washington where a drift of the belated winter was glimmering, now at the end of July, in a fold of the pachydermal slope. She had always to play some such comedy with herself before she could reconcile herself to the inevitable; and her husband was content to have her do so, as long as her drama did not involve his complexity with the inevitable. But the wildest stroke of her imagination could not inculpate him in the present affair; and though she felt it somewhat guilty of him to attempt any palliation of Lillias Bellard's behavior, she also felt it kind, and was very good to him the whole day on account of it; so that he was able honestly to pity her for the base of real tragedy he knew in her comedy. They had not only sold The Surges, where they had spent twenty summers, because of the heavy drain of hospitality upon her energies there, but because they had been offered a very good price for it, and they believed that the air of the mountains would be better for their rheumatisms. It formed at any rate a more decided change from the air of Boston; and the sale of The Surges was not altogether that sacrifice to solitude which her passionate resentment of the first menace of it had made it seem to her. Still there were associations with the things brought from the seaside cottage which supported her in the change, and which now burdened her with unavailing suggestions of how easy it would have been to make Lillias have a nice time in the more familiar environment. She sighed to herself in owning that she did not know what she should do with the girl where they were; for already, as she went through the house, she forgot her own hardship in realizing how difficult, with only the Saco

Shore House to draw upon, it would be to amuse the child.

It was an essential part of her comedy to keep this transmutation of moods from Crombie; her self-respect required it, and experience had taught her that the most generous of men would take a mean advantage if he could, and would turn from pitying to mocking her for the change. There was no outward change from the effect of plaintive submission into which she had sunk by their one-o'clock dinner-time, when, in the later afternoon she asked him to take her adrive: the last, she predicted, they should have alone together that summer. Some part of the way she dedicated to a decent pathos in the presence of scenery endeared by their unmolested meanderings, and the thought of the sweet intimacy in which they had all but got back their young married selves. But the time and the place came when she could stand it no longer, and he was hardly surprised to have her break out with the un-related conjecture, "I wonder what she *has* got up her sleeve."

"A young man, probably," he suggested.

"Don't be coarse! What makes you think that?"

"I don't know that I think that, or any-thing. What's the use of worrying about it? She'll be here so soon."

"Well, I really believe she has. And I shall watch her, I can tell you. If Aggie Bellard"—Mrs Crombie branched away in the direction of the girl's mother—"thinks she can go off to Europe for the summer, and leave Lillias scattered broadcast over the continent, with no one to look after her, she is very much mistaken." This was the ex-pression of such very complex feeling that Crombie could reply with nothing so well as a spluttering laugh. His wife knew perfectly what his laugh meant, and she went on: "I never approved of her second marriage, anyway, and I am not going to have Lillias shouldered off on me to make room for a second family in her mother's house. Archibald!" she cried, and she had to use him very sternly in the tone she was really taking with her sister and niece, "do you suppose it's a plot between them to get Lillias here with us, so that she can ingratiate herself with me, and just keep staying on indefinitely? Because if you do," she continued to threaten him, while she cast about in her mind for a penalty severe enough to fit the offence, "I won't have it!"

This was so ineffective that he had to laugh again, but he reconciled her to his derision by the real compassion with which he said, "You know you don't suppose anything of the kind yourself. It's a perfectly simple case, and the only reasonable conjecture is that Lillias has told you the exact truth in her letter. She is coming here because she has nowhere else to put in the time till the Mellays are ready for her, and in a week she will be gone. I don't think that will make any serious break in the quiet of our summer. At any rate, you can't help yourself."

"No, I can't," Mrs. Crombie recognized. "But if she imagines that she is going to hoodwink me!"

She did not attempt to say what she would do in such an event, and her husband felt no anxiety as to the sort of time Lillias would have under his roof.

T HE maid met them on their return with word that a gentleman had called while they were away. On rigid question from Mrs. Crombie she confessed that he seemed rather short and fair, but this proved to be partially an effect from Mrs. Crombie's displeasure with his being first long and dark. The girl was quite sure that he had a mustache, though she afterwards corrected herself so far as to say that his hair was cut close. He had asked for no one but Mr. Crombie, who evinced so little interest in his visitor that after a casual glance at his card he left it to the scrutiny by which his wife sought to divine him from it. From evidences not apparent to Crombie, she had decided that it was an English card, and that Mr. Edmund Craybourne was English himself, because he had no middle name, not even a middle initial.

"Did he leave any message?" She now turned upon the maid again.

"No, ma'am."

"Did he say he would come back?"

"He didn't say, m'm."

"Did he tell you whether he was stopping at the Saco Shore House?"

"He didn't tell anything, m'm."

With these facts in hand, Mrs. Crombie followed her husband to his room, where he was washing the odor of his driving-gloves from his hands, and asked him what he had to say now about Lillias Bellard.

"Well, when I said there was a young man in question, you told me not to be indecent."

"'Coarse,' I said; and it *was* coarse. Do you suppose this is the young man?"

"Not if there is none."

"Well, I know it is. Now what are you going to do? He didn't say where he was staying, and you will have to wait till he comes back. But what will you do, then?"

"I will settle that when I see him," Crombie said, applying himself vigorously to the towel. "If he is short and fair and fat, I may fall upon him and rend him; but if he is long and lank and dark, I may consider about it; though I don't know why I should do anything at all, come to think of it."

"No," Mrs. Crombie allowed, "*I* don't know why you should. In fact, I should prefer to see him myself. I could get it out of him better."

She did not say what it was, and the whole situation was simplified, as to action, by the young man's not coming back, though it was intensified as a mystery by his failure to reappear. In this aspect it supplied Mrs. Crombie with conversation quite to the end of supper, when the barge of the Saco Shore House drove up, and left Lillias Bellard and her baggage at the cottage door. Her aunt welcomed her with a warmth which she could not have imagined of herself, and affectionately ignored the girl's excuses for coming so much sooner than she had said, and so much later; for the train that brought her twenty-four hours ahead of time was a whole hour behind. For that reason she sat down to her retarded supper nearly a day before she should have had any supper at all. Her justification was that she had found people she knew coming on, and she had thought it best to come with them, hoping it would not make too much difference to her aunt Hester.

She was a pretty girl of what Crombie in his quality of incomplete artist decided was a silvery type, singularly paintable in the relation of her gray-green eyes to the argent tones of her travelling-costume, her hat and ribbons and her gloves. You must take her,

of course, with the same intention and intelligence that she had taken herself with,
or as much of it as you could get; for it was
clear that she was dressed in the frankest
sympathy with her own coloring, and in conscious rejection of all mistaken notions of
contrast. If some girls made you think of
May and others of July or August, the month
that she made you think of was September:
not the moods in which it mirrored the
coming October, but those in which it suggested the youngest months of summer, or
even spring. She was fairly mature, as he
knew from his acquaintance with her history;
she would not see twenty-seven again; but
she gave you the same sort of contradictory
impressions of youth and age that she gave
you of knowingness and innocence, of self-
reliance and helplessness, of ignorance and
experience, and of energy that ended in in-
decision.

Crombie revolved these things in his mind,

while he looked at her where she sat at table,
talking with her aunt in a serenity like that
of a September afternoon: her silvery veil
misting her gray hat above her hair, sprin-
kled even at her age with gray, and her gray
gloves lying beside her plate, physically but
not spiritually detached from her gray cos-
tume. Her intelligent eyes, glancing from
her aunt to him and back again to her, had
lovely skyey lights in them, of the sort that
haunt the horizons of the passing summer,
when the deep turquoise of the upper heav-
ens changes into the delicate emerald that
seems a reflection of the green earth below.
It struck him that if it were really a question
of his wife's knowing what her niece had up
her sleeve, she would know no more than her
niece chose to show; and if there were possi-
bilities of her being quite willing to bare both
her pretty arms to the elbows it might be
in the confident skill with which the presti-
digitator chooses to convince the witness

that there is really nothing of preparation for the feat he is about to perform, in order to heighten the effect of it.

A sense of her contradictions persisted when she rose from the table and stood not so high as he had expected, and again when she followed her aunt up-stairs with a deceptive show of height from the skirt that trailed behind her. He was shut from the revelation of the slight and rather small figure which Lillias made to Mrs. Crombie, in her room, when she had reduced herself to the fact by putting off her jacket and hat, and stood waiting in her shirt-waist for her aunt to finish explaining why she gave her that room and not another. Mrs. Crombie ended by saying that she supposed Lillias must be very tired, and would want to be going to bed; but Lillias answered, not at all, and would not her aunt sit down? She said that one got so used to distances in the West that trains rather rested one than not. Besides,

she had enjoyed a season of such entire vege-
tation, since Commencement, out on the
Pacific coast, that a little fatigue would be
an agreeable variety which she would be
glad to be aware of. At the same time she
hid a yawn with such skill that it made her
aunt respect her, and resolve to spare her as
soon as she got what she wished out of her.

She sat down provisionally and asked
Lillias whether she was going back there in
the fall, and when the girl said she did not
know but she was, Mrs. Crombie said it
must be very queer, co-education. "Aren't
they apt to get married?" she asked, with
a frown of polite disgust.

"Well, yes, they are," Lillias admitted.
"But that isn't considered such a very bad
thing, out there. You might say that there
was a good deal of courting, but there is very
little flirting; and there is nothing that is so
instantly sat upon by the girls themselves as
the least fastness. But *I* don't come in on

the question anywhere. I'm 'one of the faculty,' but my professorship, if it's that, is teaching the advanced pupils of the upper-grade schools that form part of the university. My undergraduate classes average about fourteen for girls, and fifteen or sixteen for boys, and there hasn't been a marriage among them for the whole year past. My postgraduate lecture audiences are mostly made up of townspeople who are married already."

She smiled very amusingly upon her aunt at the end of a speech which she made with pretty turns of her head and a final droop of her shoulders and a forward thrust of her chin above her hands fallen into each other in her lap. It was very young-ladyish, and as little academical as could be, so that her aunt, who had feared among other things that the child was going to be priggish, was entirely consoled. Lillias was in the department of oratory, and she might have been

expected to have a public manner, or an elo-
cutionary manner, but anything more private
or colloquial than her manner Mrs. Crombie
had not seen.   It was with the determination
not to be overcome by the peculiar charm
which she felt in her, and yet not to use unnecessary violence in avoiding the dust
which Lillias might attempt to throw into
her eyes, that Mrs. Crombie now no longer
delayed coming down to business.

"Lillias," she said, with a skirmishing
laugh, and trying not to say it with any
change of note, "we have had a very strange
call this afternoon.   Some gentleman whom
we don't at all know asked for Mr. Crombie,
while we were driving, and left his card.   We
thought perhaps he was an acquaintance of
yours, or it may be some mistake of his;
though the maid was very sure that he asked
for Mr. Crombie by name."

Mrs. Crombie gave Lillias Mr. Craybourne's
card, and that girl looked at it with a care-

lessness which only partially faded from her manner as she read. She said, "Really!" and she might apparently have contented herself with that brief comment if her aunt had not prompted her.

"You know him?"

"Yes," Lillias said, promptly enough.

Mrs. Crombie, as lightly and brightly as she could, suggested, "And you expected him?"

Lillias laughed after a little absence and silence, "Well, not quite so *soon*, Aunt Hester. I didn't expect him for a day or two yet. I won't let him bother you."

"Oh," Mrs. Crombie said, with a flight of generous insincerity, "any friend of yours!" and she prepared, with an effect of going away, which did not even lift her out of her chair, to make her next approach still more delicately. "We thought, somehow, that he was an Englishman."

The candor of Lillias in replying could not

have been greater if she was actually trying to conceal something. "Well, he *is*, Aunt Hester. He's one of those younger sons who rather abound out there."

"Oh, indeed! And the eldest son—" It was a little too leading, even with the abrupt stop that Mrs. Crombie made.

"Isn't a title, in this case. But there's property, and Mr. Craybourne's brother got it all, I guess, except the money that Mr. Craybourne has spent in amateur ranching. He's very nice, I may as well tell you at once, Aunt Hester. He's cultivated and well-read and well-mannered. *Our* men have no manners, though some of them will have when my boys grow up through the department of applied conduct, which is really my job, though I pretend to teach the niceties of speech and pronunciation only. Yes, I like Mr. Craybourne very, very much," Lillias concluded, and she remained looking at the card in her left palm, as if it were the sort of photograph that used to be called a *carte-de-visite*.

Mrs. Crombie made several attempts to speak, which ended, as they began, in gasps, and left Lillias to go on, as she did, thoughtfully.

"He is very nice, and very bidable, though what he might be *afterwards!*—"

Now, indeed, Mrs. Crombie broke from her inarticulate struggles. "Why, Lillias Bellard, are you engaged to Mr. Craybourne?"

"Well, no. But we're *seeing*."

III

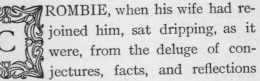ROMBIE, when his wife had re-joined him, sat dripping, as it were, from the deluge of conjectures, facts, and reflections which she had hastened to pour out on him after coming away from Lillias.

"Anything more outspoken, more bold-faced, more unblushing! If *those* are the manners that she is teaching the youth out there under the guise of elocution!"

"There does seem to be a sort of brazen ingenuousness in it," Crombie allowed. "But you can't say there's anything deceitful. And that's what you dreaded."

"I don't know whether I dreaded it. But I did hope that if Lillias *had* anything to conceal she would manage it with a little finesse,

26

a little delicacy. I hoped that if she was going to bring the burden of a love-affair into the house with her, she would have the grace to carry it off so that it shouldn't seem to be a burden. But the brutal frankness with which she dumps it all on me!"

"I don't call it brutal," Crombie said, with an air of reasoning, "though it is certainly frank. I think it has its charm. It's deliciously honest, and it ought to be a relief to you, after the duplicity you've been dreading—the finesse, as you call it."

"I call it duplicity, pretending to come here for a week, so as to bridge over between visits, and meaning all the time to make us a base of operations, with him at the Saco Shore House, so that they can see each other constantly under my very wing. If that isn't finesse, I don't know what it is!"

"Then, I don't see what you have to complain of, with frankness and finesse both on hand in one and the same Mephistophelian innocent."

"Oh, Archie!" Mrs. Crombie whimpered. "It's the care! It's the terrible disappointment of a broken-up summer! It's having the disturbance of it going on under our roof day after day, when I was looking forward to such a complete rest with you, dear! It's enough to make me wish we were back at The Surges. You had better sell this place at once."

"There'll be time enough to think about that and to change our minds twice or thrice. Mountain property hasn't the instant convertibility of shore property. I should find some difficulty in giving this place away if I was in a hurry to get rid of it. Fortunately I'm not. Did she tell you how they happened to meet?"

"Oh, romantically enough, I believe. After his last failure in ranching he was quite at leisure, and he came into town to pass the time at the hotel, and think. There he heard of Lillias's lectures, or talks, which were open to the public—really, I can't imagine it, but her lectures seem to be quite a fad, out there—and he went to one of them, and then he went to all that were left of them. At last he got himself introduced; though why he didn't at first she couldn't understand, unless it was his English shyness. After he did it seems to have been plain sailing, as far as they've gone."

"And how far have they gone?"

"Well, she doesn't seem to know, exactly. The case appears to be that she has some doubts of marriage itself."

"Oh, come, now! A pretty girl like that?"

"I don't see what her prettiness has to do with it. A great many girls are that way, now. They look at it very cool-headedly. They don't like to give up their liberty unless they're certain of their happiness, and they

see, if they look round them at all, that
there's a great deal of unhappiness in marriage."

"They could always get divorced."

"Yes, but they don't like that—nice girls
don't. They'd rather not go in for it, to
begin with. It seems that Lillias has a
great idea of being honest with herself.
Really, to hear her talk— I wish you could
have been at the key-hole!"

"I wish I could—if I may be as honest as
Lillias."

"It seems that it wasn't the hard work,
or the beginning at the bottom, or the personal exhibition, as Mrs. Kemble calls it,
which kept her from going on the stage.
There was a manager quite ready to take her
from the dramatic school and feature her, as
she said, in a new play—"

"Don't go too far back!"

"I'm not, but you can't understand if I
don't.—It was the perpetual pretence; what

she felt was the essential and final falsity of a life that consisted in the representation of emotions that were not really felt. In short, the insincerity."

"Well?"

"Well—where was I? Oh yes! She felt that if she had no doubt about marrying Mr. Craybourne she would have no misgivings about marriage; or if she had perfect faith in marriage she could confidently trust herself in marrying him. But as she has neither, she can't."

Crombie rubbed his forehead, as if to clear away a cloud within. "I don't believe I've followed you," he said.

"Why, he's offered himself, but she hasn't thought it out yet."

"And she's got him here to help her think?"

"That is where the sinuosity comes in; that is where Lillias shows herself a true girl."

Crombie laughed. "And what does she expect us to do?"

"Do you know what she said to me? Not just in so many words, but that was the sum and substance of it. She made a long, sly preamble about having always thought us the happiest married couple she had ever seen, the most united and harmonious; and she wanted Mr. Craybourne to know us, too."

"As a sort of object-lesson? I'm not sure that I should like to be studied. It would make me conscious."

"Of course," Mrs. Crombie said, with a seriousness which amazed him, "it's very flattering."

"It's taffy of the most barefaced description. Now, my dear, you look out for that girl. Don't trust her beyond your sight. Does she expect us to take any active part in regard to this Englishman of hers?"

"Oh no. And I quite agree with you

about her slyness. There can't be so much
smoke without some fire, and I shall certainly watch her. She wants to commit us
to some scheme in her mother's absence, and
I am not going to be used. She will find
that out."

The talk of the Crombies ended for the
night in a very exhaustive analysis of the
relations of Lillias to her more immediate
family, then as remote in space as close in
blood, and in a just recognition of how very
little the girl, left to shift for herself, owed
her mother in obedience or deference. Mrs.
Crombie led the conclusion in censure of her
sister, with those reserves in behalf of her
peculiarities which a woman sometimes likes
to make in judging her next of kin, as if their
eccentricities somehow reflected picturesque-
ness if not praise upon herself. Lillias, she
said, had come honestly by anything that
was original in her; and she did not know
but that if the girl was now hesitating in a

way that was ridiculous about accepting
Mr. Craybourne, she was certainly improv-
ing upon her mother, who used to be always
hesitating about people after she had accepted them, and sometimes after she had
married them. In the case of Lillias's
father, she reminded Crombie, Aggie's mis-
giving had gone so far as to have the character of a provisional separation for a whole
year before his death. She asked Crombie
if he did not think that this showed a real
honesty in the child; and he said that he did.
By this time he was so sleepy that he would
have said anything.

He was quite as compliant when he woke,
but he found his wife of another mind, after
a night passed beyond the influence of her
niece. She came into his room before he
was up, or fairly awake, fully dressed and
with a defensive armor invisibly on, which
she betrayed in saying, "Well, she is a case."

"Why, what has she been doing now?"

Crombie asked, instantly roused to consciousness.

"Oh, nothing. I have just been thinking her over, and I have gone back to my first impressions. I think what she has done is enough without anything more. The question is, what ought we to do? Shall we quietly ignore Mr. Craybourne until she chooses to make a move, or shall we ignore her, and you go over to the Saco Shore and call upon him, and take the bull by the horns? Do you know, my dear, I believe that's just what she wants you to do. How can we tell but it's a plot between them to force our hands? There's every probability, to my mind, that she planned for him to get here before her, so that he would come and be looked over before she arrived, and we be driven at the point of the bayonet to say what we think of him. I'll bet anything you dare that she was enraged beyond description when she found that she had missed fire, and that we hadn't seen him, after all!"

"I don't think it's fair," Crombie said, "to use such various and vigorous imagery with a man that's still on his back."

"Well, you must get up, then." She had been going about, pulling up window-shades and throwing open shutters, as she talked, and she now confronted him in the full light of day. "It's nearly breakfast-time, anyway; and I want to talk it thoroughly over with you after you're shaved."

"I shall be clearer, then; but I shall be a great deal hungrier, and I don't believe I can talk it over till I've had my coffee."

"You've got to," she said, going out of the room.

But before he had half finished shaving, and while he was still grieving inwardly at having to help his wife make up her mind about her niece all over again, he heard her voice gayly lifted and the clash of enthusiastic kisses in a pause of the rustling skirts that he knew to be meeting in the upper hallway on which all the bedroom doors opened. He noticed that his wife's and her niece's voices were very much alike in the one asking, "Why, child, you poor thing, are you up already? Why didn't you let me send your breakfast to your room?" and the other answering, "Oh, I'm always up to breakfast, aunt, and I'm so be-you-tifully rested, I couldn't think of it."

"Well, then, come right down. It 'll be on the table instantly," he heard his wife continue. "Your uncle will come any old time, as he says, and we needn't wait for him."

"Well, I *am* rather nippish," he heard Lillias owning in the same note.

The girl was very amusing, he thought, when he found them at breakfast, and Mrs. Crombie said she had been telling about her university life, out there, and bade her go on.

"Oh, I don't believe Uncle Archibald will care for it," Lillias said, but she corrected herself so far as to add, "It *is* rather funny, I suppose, to you, off here." He liked her standing up so for her adoptive West, and he showed an immediate interest which inspired her. She was looking still prettier than the night before, and the flower-like freshness of her morning-dress was quite as becoming as the twilight tones which had clothed her as with a pensive music the night before. He tried to put out of his mind a saying to the effect that in the dark all cats are gray, while he found a singular pleasure in the pseudo-deference with which she addressed herself to him. "You see," she continued, "that my lectures are rather outside of the regular courses, and that was the reason why the general public was always more or less at them. I believe they were popular, but I knew all the time that they would have been more popular if they had been more — well, humbuggy. And you know I couldn't stand that, uncle," she appealed to him with a sidelong glance.

" No," he assented, in a way that made her laugh.

She went on: "People like that, both old and young, and I should have had all the unoccupied human material that goes into women's clubs raving about me, if I had done some sort of Delsarte business; they would have much preferred a song and dance to the modesty of nature which I was trying to brag up by precept and practice. I was tolerably adored by my classes, as it was, but I should have had them in ecstasies if I had descended to the cheap kind of things we were taught to avoid in the dramatic school."

"Yes," Crombie said, and now Lillias did not immediately continue.

When she did, it was to say, with a silently accumulated frankness, "The only one, really, that thoroughly understood, from the first instant, what I was driving at, was Mr. Craybourne. I suppose," she said, with another cast of her eyes, though this time it was rather defiant than appealing, towards Crombie, "Aunt Hester has told you about *him?*"

"Not at all! What about him?"

His effrontery made her laugh again.

"Oh, that's another story, as Kipling says —or used to say; I believe he doesn't say it now, any more. This story only relates to his telling me, as soon as he could manage to get introduced—which he did by very properly waiting and asking the president to perform the ceremony, when he could have got any soul in the place to do it at once—that I was the first person to give him the least notion of what nature was at."

"Indeed!" Crombie said. "Did you believe him?"

"Not immediately. There's nothing," she

deferred, "that we suspect so much as downright openness, is there?"

"It's often very misleading."

"Well, I found out afterwards that he really meant it. That," she added, after a distinct interval, "was what gave me pause," and Crombie felt that she had come to the other story. "There is no use beating about the bush, and I'm not going to. Aunt Hester," she now turned to Mrs. Crombie, "I may as well say first as last that if the Mellays hadn't providentially written to put me off a week I should have invented some providential excuse for coming to you and letting me meet Mr. Craybourne as nearly on the parental premises as I could get them."

Crombie stole a look at his wife, but he could detect nothing of resentment in her face; nothing but a generous and protecting welcome. She laid her left hand along the table towards the girl, and Lillias put hers gratefully into it. "You have done exactly right, my dear," she said, and Lillias went on, piecing a little break in her voice:

"Even if mother were on the ground, and not off in the wilds of Europe somewhere, I should wish Uncle Archie's approval, as I've no father of my own; for in the kind of scrambling life I've led I like to have a thing of this kind perfectly regular. I'm not the least bit bohemian, Aunt Hester, though I know you always thought me so—"

"No, my dear!" Mrs. Crombie protested, but Lillias tenderly insisted:

"Oh yes, you did, aunt, and I don't blame you; I should have, myself. But at heart I'm deadly respectable, and Mr. Craybourne's being an Englishman makes me all the more anxious to be more so; though he thinks the other kind of thing is charming, and was quite ready to be fetched by it—at least in my case. You see, I'm not having any concealments from you!"

"You needn't have, poor child!" Mrs.

Crombie said, so tenderly that Crombie kept himself with difficulty from a derisory snort.

"And now you have the whole thing before you. I have come to you simply for a social basis, a domestic hearth, a family fireside, and when Mr. Craybourne comes I want him to find me in a chimney-corner belonging to my own kith and kin."

The terms of this declaration, and the mixed tones in which it was delivered, were such as to make Crombie feel that it need not be taken too seriously, though it could not be taken too earnestly; so, when his wife, with an adjuratory frown, indicated that it was for him, as head of the house, to make their joint response, he said, with a certain hardy gayety:

"And when *is* he coming?"

"Oh, any moment!" Lillias said, with a rueful little smile full of gladness at his light daring. "That is, if one can judge from his already being here before me. I suppose I may say that it wasn't his fault that we are not here on our wedding journey."

She turned from her uncle to her aunt in making this observation, and Mrs. Crombie met it in the same spirit. "Well, Lillias, I must say that you have done very wisely in the whole matter. I should never have forgiven myself if any fancied inconvenience to us had kept you from coming to us in such an emergency; and no matter how it turns out, I shall write to Aggie that you have done everything that a girl could do."

"Thank you, Aunt Hester," and the two women had a moment of mothering and daughtering in which Crombie could not join them.

"Well, I am prepared to do anything you want," he said, with an ironical ease, and a genuine interest in the affair which he thought it more manly to conceal. "Do I understand that Mr. Craybourne will ask for me again?"

44

Miss Bellard's Inspiration

"Yes, indeed!" the girl said. "We are not out there now, and he knows it."

"And what am I to say, when he asks to see you—if he does?"

Lillias looked at her aunt, who visibly failed to formulate a line of conduct for Crombie, and then she looked back at him, and said, caressingly, "Oh, just trust to the inspiration of the moment, uncle."

"Then you leave it all to me?"

"Quite."

"Well, I've never had the chance of forbidding a young man my house before, and perhaps I sha'n't do it in just the way that this Mr. Craybourne is used to, but I think I can do it effectually."

Crombie wore the mustache of his period branching into the side whiskers of the early eighteen-sixties, and it was with a fine flare of both that he now tilted his head on one side and waited for his wife and niece to precede him out of the breakfast-room. His

45

beard and the gossamer traces of his hair were faded from their earlier red to an agreeable yellowish white, and his bulging blue eyes matched very well with them and with a complexion of ancestral Scotch floridity, so that as he stood leaning forward with his thumbs in his waistcoat-pockets he was such a fine elderly Du Maurier military type that Lillias could hardly forbear throwing him a kiss. She did forbear, but she forbore with a backward roll of her own eyes which had all the effect of a thrown kiss. "You'll be splendid, Uncle Archie, whatever you do," she encouraged him, though it made him tremble, almost, to see her put her arm round her aunt's waist. He felt that she might carry it too far in constituting herself Mrs. Crombie's protégée, and in fact he fancied Mrs. Crombie's waist tacitly stiffening under the caress.

To make sure, he asked her, when Lillias had gone up to her room for a moment,

Miss Bellard's Inspiration

"Then you've changed your mind about her?"

"Not at all!" his wife returned, in the scorn often used by women to give dignity to a misstatement. "I feel exactly as I did, though in an entirely different way. She is not underhanded, but overhanded, and she thinks that if she is perfectly transparent I shall not see through her. All is, I shall have to fight her in the open."

"Where did you get that expression?" Crombie parleyed.

"I don't know: in some of those English South African accounts. You know what I mean. She is determined to be married from this house."

Crombie caught his breath, and then whistled.

"I can see it," she went on, "as plain as the nose on my face. But I can tell her she won't do it, without my knowing it."

Miss Bellard's Inspiration

"I wish I knew what you meant by that," Crombie sighed.

"Well, you will see."

Just then Lillias's trailing skirts were heard on the stairs like the drift of fallen leaves down a forest path.

IV

M R. CRAYBOURNE, whatever were his impulses to an earlier call, had quelled them so far as not to come before eleven o'clock in the morning, though why he should have come before the afternoon can be explained only on the ground that the country informality and the summer heat had relaxed him to a social freedom which he might not otherwise have permitted himself. When he did come, however, he was not relaxed to the extreme of asking for Miss Bellard. He asked for Mr. Crombie, and he was shown to him in the library, a room that few men could have had so little need of as the master of the house. It had some books, mostly dishevelled paper copies of novels, tumbling about on its shelves; and it was stuck round with Crombie's sketches on pasteboard and canvas, memories of The Surges and its scenery, and forecasts of the White Mountain landscape, and bits of the Saco valley. Crombie was so old-fashioned in his methods that these attempts were like rejected studies by poorer masters of the extinct White Mountain school. He was ranging among them, trying, with his mouth puckered to an inaudible whistle, to make choice of some one or other that might be carried farther, when Mr. Craybourne rang. Crombie had almost forgotten about him, but he now started into a sense of him that took all nature out of his careless ease. He came forward, however, with outstretched hand, and welcomed him. He said, "Ah, how do you do, Mr. Craybourne?" in a tone of expectation that struck upon his own ear as not quite the thing; and he did not know whether he mended matters much or not by adding, "Sorry not to have been at home when you called yesterday. Sit down."

"Oh, thank you, thank you," Mr. Craybourne said, and after faltering a moment on foot he folded himself down and down, by what appeared to Crombie successive plications, into the rather low chair appointed him. The result of the process brought his face somewhat more on a level with Crombie's, who was himself of such a good height that he was at least not used to being towered over, and who saw that Mr. Craybourne's face was a decidedly handsome, tanned face, regular in feature, with rather deep-set blue eyes, and a skin burnished on the cheeks, chin, and upper lip by the very close shave which the barber at the Saco Shore House had just given him. He diffused, involuntarily, as Crombie decided, a faint and fainter odor of the bay-rum which he had not been quick enough to keep the barber from dabbling him with after the close shave; and he also seemed to have a good deal of wrist, from which, on the right and left, he nervously clasped his hat with slender, gentlemanly hands. His hands had been liberated from the labor of the fields by the failure of his ranching experiment so long as to have lost the brown of the sun and wind, but they had the tone of his complexion. The clasp he had given Crombie was soft, yet firm, and not at all damp, in spite of the nervousness that brought some perspiration to the young man's straight, comely forehead.

The embarrassing variety of topics which Crombie had to choose from, in view of the intimate relations he found himself in with this perfect stranger through the frankness of Lillias Bellard, kept him silent for a breath or two. Then he said, "Fine day."

"Yes," Mr. Craybourne admitted, with an indrawn sigh, as if from the sense of reprieve. "But I suppose you expect fine weather at this time of year."

Miss Bellard's Inspiration

Crombie saw his opening and said, "Yes, rather oftener than we get it," and this made way for a mutual smile of such good-fellowship that it was easy for him to add, "I suppose I needn't conceal that I know you wish to ask for Miss Bellard." Mr. Craybourne could apparently do no more than laugh gratefully, and Crombie said, "She came last night, you know."

"Yes, I know. I—I had the pleasure of seeing her at the station," the young man innocently said, and Crombie concealed any surprise he felt at having ascertained a limit to Lillias Bellard's frankness, which had seemed so unbounded. In fact, for a few seconds he felt no surprise, or anything at all, the effect of Mr. Craybourne's simple statement was so benumbing. Then abysms of astonishment began to open within him, to which there was no bottom. Had the girl meant to tell her aunt of this meeting, and had the moment slipped by her in her first grapple with the fact of Craybourne's presence, and got so far by that she could not overtake it? If she had meant to keep their meeting a secret, why had not she charged Craybourne not to speak of it? There was mystery here which Crombie's plummet could not fathom, and before which he shuddered in conjecture, while he smiled to think how completely his wife had been taken in by her niece. He first abhorred the girl's duplicity, and then his abhorrence yielded to pity for the unknown necessity which had forced her to it, and at the same time his bare scalp felt the ghost of its vanished hair rise on it at the thought of what Mrs. Crombie might do and say when she found out the fact.

"Oh, I didn't know you met her," he said, hollowly, and not very wisely.

"I said *saw*," the young man returned. "I don't think she saw *me*. I didn't speak with her; she preferred that we should meet first at your house. That is why I—I have come so unwarrantably early."

Crombie had two reasons for falling upon the young man: one, resentment for having been so misled, and the other relief for being rescued from the error, which, now it was gone, he knew must have left him without a shred of respect for the poor child whose difficult little romance had enlisted his interest. But he spared his guest, and mercly said, "Oh, I see!" and smiled fatuously, in adding, "I *thought* it was rather odd she hadn't mentioned it. Ah, ha, ha!" he ended, in rehearsal of the merriment of a man laughing to his wife at a good joke on himself. He experienced such a kindly revulsion toward Lillias, whom he had wronged by his error, that he could not bear any longer to keep her from her happiness in her lover's presence. "If you will excuse me," he said, with a politeness that was almost tender, "I will tell the ladies you are here."

Miss Bellard's Inspiration

He was moving toward the door when he was arrested by a "Well—ah—well," from Mr. Craybourne, which sounded like the preliminary of an entreaty for a stay of action. He turned, and the young man, still crouching over his hat, made a more successful effort for coherence, "I really oughtn't to see Miss Bellard—or, I should say, Mrs. Crombie—till I have given you some notion of how matters stand with us — Miss Bellard, I mean. I don't know what Miss Bellard has said, or whether she has told you how entirely I am without claim on her?"

Crombie rather liked this, which he thought manly, but he could only say, "Oh, we quite understand that it's only in the *pour parler* stage, and nobody's committed." That was the year of the Spanish War, and every one spoke more or less in the diplomatic French of the opening negotiations for peace; the papers all had a touch of it.

The Englishman returned with a certain

stiffness of self-assertion against the prompt American pliability of his host, " You're very good, I'm sure. But I can't allow you to suppose that *I* am not committed. If I had not felt myself so absolutely committed from the moment I first heard Miss Bellard speak, and first saw her, I should not have felt at liberty to address her, in the absence of her natural—her family. Of course, I had the countenance of the president of the university; I had the honor of an introduction from him; but it was the other — feeling that seemed to warrant me in—ah—going on." The young man spoke with courage, but not steadily; Crombie noticed with a mixture of pathos and amusement that his chin was trembling.

"Oh yes. Quite right. I meant that *she* was not committed—"

"No," the Englishman said, "and I am prepared now, if Mrs. Crombie thinks there has been anything irregular in my—my—

procedure, to go away without seeing Miss Bellard, and wait till her mother returns; though I believe that is rather indefinite. Not that I couldn't wait indefinitely."

Crombie had a notion of not being out-done in punctiliousness, if it came to that, and he put on the air of giving the matter thought. "She would want her mother's approval, naturally. But—I don't think it's necessary for you to go away. In fact"— he caught at the inspiration—"Mrs. Crombie was rather hoping you would stay to lunch."

"Why, you're very good," Craybourne said. "I'm sure I shall be very glad if— But I should like, if it won't bore you, or if you won't think it unnecessary—to tell you— I don't know whether she has told you— that I have formally offered myself to Miss Bellard. It came to that very soon. Am I tiring you? Are you interested?"

"Oh, quite. Not at all, I assure you. Go on!" Crombie, in token of his patience and

Miss Bellard's Inspiration

concern, relapsed into the chair from which
he had risen, and took from the table a paper-
knife offering itself there to his hand.

"The whole affair has been so—different,
that I should be glad to make sure that from
the—the—from your point of view, I have
been—warranted."

Crombie bowed seriously and the Englishman went on.

"I can't say, looking back, that I was
actuated by anything better than an idle
curiosity in going, the first time, to hear Miss
Bellard lecture. I should like you to know
that; she knows it. I was at the hotel, with
nothing to do, and I heard her lectures talked
of. Not," the young man made haste to
add, "in any slighting way. But nearly
everything is a joke, out there, and I can't say
that Miss Bellard's lectures were taken very
seriously by the hotel acquaintance who mentioned them: he spoke of them as a good
show; he has apologized and explained that

he meant nothing derogatory. They were very popular. Ah — have you — you have heard her—lecture?"

Crombie shook his head. "She took it up, I've understood, after leaving the dramatic school, as a means of—independence. We did not know of it till we heard of her appointment to a lectureship, out there. I must confess we had our misgivings."

The young man ardently cried, "You needn't have had! Anything more graceful, more beautiful, more natural, more artistic, more divine—" He stopped for want of words, and then resumed at another point. "I will say, that I was chiefly interested, as far as I was worthily interested, by the fact, which I heard, that Miss Bellard was doing it for, as you say, independence. You may think it odd, and you may not agree with me at all, but I go in for women doing that kind of thing. I suppose that I might be considered an extremist by some people.

But I believe that marriage would be happier, generally speaking, if the wife and husband were always pecuniarily independent of each other."

Crombie thought that he had heard of some marriages, especially international marriages, in which the wife alone had the means of pecuniary independence, but he could not note these instances, even in the way of jest, to the eager and ingenuous countenance of his visitor. He murmured, "Quite so," and Mr. Craybourne went on.

"I am happy to say that Miss Bellard and I are of the same opinion on this point. In fact, it was the very first point that came up for discussion between us, and it was she who urged it first."

It seemed, hazily enough, to Crombie's intelligence, that the young pair who could have reached this point in their love-making, without anything more definite than the girl's consent to be made love to, were mod-

ern beyond any *fin-de-siècle* newness of the
century then ending; but it was easier not to
grasp the fact, and he did not grasp it, at
least very firmly. Hazily, also, he conceived
of the young man's liberal-mindedness as a
willingness to let a wife make her own living,
which he had known carried to the excess of
letting her make her husband's living too;
but again he was unable to impart his reflections. He said, "I believe Lillias has de-
veloped in that direction since we — have
seen much of her. One finds girls feeling like
that a good deal, nowadays."

"Yes," the young man assented, "but not
quite in her way, I believe." He seemed
proud of her singularity, and jealous of its
attribution to any one else. "I don't know,"
he continued, "whether I can explain—and
in fact it's only in the most provisional way
that I can allow myself to talk of it at all—
how this breadth of view—it's a kind of cant,
but I don't find just the words I want—

added to the charm she had for me from the
first moment. I understood, when I first
saw her, that I saw her earning her living;
and later I was told that she had prepared
herself to earn her living on the stage. It
was impossible for me, from the beginning,
not to think of how I should feel toward such
a fact if she were my wife; I don't justify my
presumption, because it was in no degree
voluntary: the case, as it were, supposed itself, and I did ask myself the question on
these very indefensible grounds. There could
only be one answer. I ought to say that I
had read myself and thought myself out of the
prejudices of what I should once have called
my class, and I could feel nothing but admira-
tion and reverence for her—her attitude."

The young man's words flowed rapidly
enough, but there had not ceased to be in
their stream that tremor, that vibrant eager-
ness which had moved Crombie. He pricked
up his thin red ears at the spare allusion to

Miss Bellard's Inspiration

Mr. Craybourne's social rank, a thing which the true American prefers even in the Englishman who renounces it, especially if the Englishman is seeking an alliance with his family; yet the liking with which this Mr. Craybourne had inspired him was not mean. It was merely qualified with a satisfaction in his being socially a gentleman, which he would not have exacted from an American pretendant; such a pretendant would have been wholly left to the instinct and knowledge of the girl in that case.

He now merely said, "That's all right, Mr. Craybourne. It's a matter for you to settle with Lillias. In fact, with a girl who has been taking care of herself for the last year or two, I should be a little shy of interfering in any way. But she has a feeling, which we consider a very right one, that—that if she's got some thinking over to do, she had better do it under her family roof, or as nearly as she can come to one."

Here, Crombie had got to the end of his tether, and had so literally nothing more to say that he was glad of Craybourne's eager suggestion, "Then I have your permission? I may—"

"Why, certainly," Crombie said, and again he started toward the door. "I will tell Mrs. Crombie you are here."

"A moment!" the young man interposed. "I ought to apologize perhaps for—for turning up here yesterday, before Miss Bellard's arrival—when—"

"I don't think that's a thing a girl could really object to, no matter how matters stood," Crombie said.

"I was hoping," the young man pursued, "for some such interview as this, and for the opportunity of speaking of a point on which I'm told that Americans are rather more sensitive than Englishmen. I wish to say that there is no question whatever of—of money in my mind; a *dot*, or that kind of thing. If the time ever came when Miss Bellard chose to abandon her independent career, there would be sufficient provision for the future. My elder brother was naturally my father's heir; but an uncle of mine left me something which I haven't quite made ducks and drakes of."

He smiled a little anxiously, and Crombie said, largely, "Oh, that's all right, Mr. Craybourne. The great thing is whether you can make up your minds to each other."

"Yes!" the young man deeply sighed. "Whether *she* can."

V

"WELL, I thoroughly like him," Mrs. Crombie said, looking at the backs of Lillias and Craybourne narrowing in the perspective as they took their way down the lane that led from the cottage grounds to the banks of the Saco. The meeting of the lovers had taken place under her eye in Crombie's library, and she had been pleased with his discreet ardor, and the girl's plain good sense. They had all sat down for some time, and then Mrs. Crombie had eliminated herself in some housekeeping interest, discovering in the act that Crombie had already disappeared. Lillias and Craybourne remained together for some time longer, when she joined her aunt up-stairs,

67

and said she had come for her hat: she was
going out with Mr. Craybourne to explore.
Mrs. Crombie bade her be sure and be back
to lunch promptly, and she now added to
Crombie, "And I like *her*. She is a good
girl."

"Almost too good to be true," Crombie
suggested cynically.

"No; I've quite changed my mind about
that. I believe Lillias is just what we see
her. What became of you so suddenly?"

"Was it sudden? I didn't seem to be
needed. I had had a good deal of him before
you came in."

"There *is* a good deal of him, in one way,"
she reflected. "He is very tall; and Lillias
is not a tall girl; she is certainly not 'new'
in *that* way. But she can manage. She
is managing now. Look at them! She is
keeping just the right distance and at the
proper angle from him, so that the difference
won't be noticed. I know that she got that

summer hat of hers so as to reduce his height."

"One would think," Crombie said, gloomily, "that you liked her illusiveness."

"She isn't illusive in the essentials; but in some things a girl *has* to be illusive; and Lillias has been left to do for herself in a great many things where most girls' mothers are illusive *for* them. I don't see how Aggie can excuse herself. But you certainly have the gift of choosing the most offensive expressions! One would think you really disliked the child. Aren't you glad to see her so happy?"

"Well, I haven't quite adjusted myself yet to having such a well-spring of pleasure turned on in the house. I haven't got over sympathizing with you at her breaking into your tranquillity."

"Yes, there is that, and it is very nice of you to remember it, but you mustn't lay it up against her. I didn't know she was going to be so interesting. She is *very* interesting. I wish you could have heard her telling all about her life out there. What made you keep us waiting so long?"

"Was she impatient? I had to let him free his mind. He wanted to tell me a lot of things. Principally that he approved of her independence, but if she ever wanted to go back on it, he had money enough for them both."

"He *has?* I don't believe Lillias knows that. And well?"

"That he doesn't expect anything with her."

"Well, that is certainly ideal! He certainly isn't a common Englishman."

"He doesn't seem to be a noble one, either. It's the noble ones that go in for the money."

"You know what I mean, and I hope Lillias will make up her mind to have him before he leaves. How long is he going to stay?"

"I didn't ask him."

"Of course not. But I thought he might have mentioned it. I'm glad, anyway, that you asked him to lunch."

"Oh, I thought I might as well have a hand in bu'sting our blissful calm."

"What's the matter with you, Archibald?" she turned on him with the demand, and he at once denied that there was anything the matter.

Whether she believed him or not, or thought that she could get it out of him better some other time, she let him be for the present, and went about seeing that luncheon should be of the signal character which befitted the occasion, and they did not meet again till they sat down at table with the young people. Crombie went out, charged to go quite in the opposite direction from that they had taken, and did one of his ridiculous sketches, which he knew himself were bad, and could hardly forgive people for pretending to admire, but which amused for him a leisure otherwise intolerable. He did not come in till quite luncheon-time, and so escaped the duty of entertaining Mr. Craybourne in the library, when Lillias had brought the young man back with her half an hour earlier, so that she could change her dress, and talk with her aunt, whom she found to be lying in wait for her.

"Come in, Aunt Hester!" she invited the hungering apparition that showed itself at her doorway, and she added with her splendid frankness, "Well, it has been a perfect land-slide."

"What do you mean? Have you accepted him?"

"No, but I am quite prepared to do so— emotionally prepared. We went over to look at the slide, across the river, by your ferry, and when I saw how it had done the work of ages, in about three minutes from the time it started, as the owner of the farm said, and covered about twenty acres with granite and gravel, and leaves ground to pulp, and logs of big trees chewed off, and packed full of sand so that you couldn't strike an axe into them, I felt just so myself. The undermining separation of the last four weeks had had its effect, and the first four minutes with him did the rest, and I should be asking your congratulations now, Aunt Hester, if it had not been for Mr. Craybourne's delicacy in giving me more time than I wanted. He is a dear, but he is making it difficult."

"Why, Lillias, I don't suppose he thinks he is allowed to speak unless he has some hint from you," Mrs. Crombie said, in high approval of him.

"Do you think so, Aunt Hester? Well, that is rather embarrassing. Is it usual for girls to hint?"

"Not unless it is absolutely necessary, my dear."

"Did you—hint?"

"Certainly not! What a question!"

"Because if you did, I think I will. I think it had better be over."

While they talked, Lillias was effecting what is called by performers in the drama where one actor takes several parts, a lightning change, and was reappearing from the pastoral simplicity of her walking-dress in the elaboration of an afternoon toilette. The change was not exactly imperative, under the circumstances, and yet both of the women felt that it was highly desirable, and were perhaps tacitly agreed that if a hint were not possible, there were means of otherwise doing its work quite as effectually. When Lillias came down to join Mr. Craybourne in the library before luncheon, and wait with him there for her aunt and uncle, she was what is known to her sex as a dream. The word is commonly used in description of a very visionary gown, but Lillias so thoroughly characterized her gown, and subdued it to her personality that she was herself the dream.

The young man glowed all over love at sight of her, and a landslide must have taken place in him too. He seized the first minutes or moments that they could have together, and huskily entreated, "Lillias, why not say it now?"

She smiled mystically, beatifically, and "Well!" she said.

Then everything was said between them, and Crombie and his wife coming in directly, Lillias told them.

There began with the whole household now a series of experiences as idyllic as any which have been put into poetry, but which would have very much the effect of prose if they were successively presented. They had for the lovers, in fact, no succession, but a sort of rapturous simultaneity, imaginable of a state of being in which the problem of time and space was eliminated. They were together, as it seemed, by mere volition, and the hotel was so near, and his presence in the Crombie cottage so constant, that there was no question to his consciousness of coming or going. Lillias knew of course that he took so many of his meals at her uncle's table that the exception was when he remained at the hotel for any of them. He got to coming over to breakfast, and with her aunt's habit of breakfasting in bed, and her uncle's way of breakfasting whenever he happened to get up, they mostly had the meal alone together. Lillias would say to Mrs. Crombie's neat waitress, "You needn't stay, Norah. I think we can take care of ourselves," and then Norah would not stay.

One morning, when Lillias and Norah had played this comedy, the young man said, with a worshipping look at the face which Lillias had given the effect of a very pretty girl's, "I suppose it will be something like this when we are really—"

He hesitated with a fine modesty, and she suggested, "*It?*"

"Yes! And what a nice, comprehensive little word!"

"You can say a good deal," she returned, thoughtfully, "with almost any sort of word when you mean it. But I was thinking," she added, "that perhaps it mightn't be always so."

"Why not?"

"Well—is your coffee just right?"

"Sweetness and strength have kissed each other in it. But why mightn't it be always so?"

"Oh, I don't know. Sometimes we might be cross. I think I am rather apt to be cross in the morning."

"I have never seen you so, Lillias!"

"You never have seen me in the morning more than half a dozen times, yet. But I suppose we shall have our little outs."

"Quarrels?"

"Yes, regular rows."

Craybourne no longer protested against the notion. He asked, "I wonder what made you think of that?"

"Why?"

"Because it was in my mind too, and I was trembling to think it mightn't be always like this."

"Probably, then, I got it out of your mind. It was a case of thought-transference." She smiled in radiant burlesque, but immediately asked, with a dangerous little inflation of the nostrils, which escaped him, "Or perhaps there was something in my behavior that suggested it to you?"

"No," he answered, so simply that the most impassioned suspicion must have been allayed in her, who saw that her suspicion was not suspected. "You are never otherwise than angelically peaceful. But—how very slight the partition walls in your summer hotels seem to be!"

"Was that what you were going to say?"

"Not at all. But it is on the way to it. I was kept awake last night by the sound of a 'regular row' in the room next mine."

"It served you right—if you were eavesdropping."

"Oh, but I wasn't. That was the odd part. I was a perfectly helpless ear-witness, as one might call it. But I am afraid I recognized their voices as those of a couple who sat at table with me at supper. The husband seemed to be interested in the view of Mr. Crombie's cottage, which he had had from the hotel veranda, and asked me if I knew who lived there. The wife manifested —what shall I say?—such an ostentatious indifference that I saw she was curious too. They had nothing to say to each other, and the question may have been merely to make conversation with a third person."

"And did you tell them?"

"I don't know why I didn't. But I evaded the question."

"You poor thing! It must have been a great strain on you—any sort of uncandor. Do you know, Edmund, I think your candor is the nicest thing about you?"

"Really? I must cultivate it."

"No, if you did I should feel that I had made you conscious, and I could never forgive myself for that. What did they say to each other?"

"Nothing."

"But when they kept you awake?"

The young man had a certain hesitation. "Well, I don't know! Wasn't it rather in the nature of a confidence? An involuntary confidence?"

"Yes, it was," Lillias admitted, with all her frankness. But she added, with a courage which fetched, "Still, if we are one—or going to be—it wouldn't be the same as if you spoke of it to another."

Miss Bellard's Inspiration

"You darling!" Craybourne started up, all his length, and asked, "May I?"

"Well," she said, "if you will be very quick."

He ran round the table, and after he had been very quick, or very much quicker than he wished, he sat down, all his length, and asked, "Where was I?"

"On the point of telling me what they said."

"It appeared to be principally names. But as far as the tenor of their discourse was coherent, it related to a separation. It was mixed up with a good deal of crying from her."

"Edmund!"

"Yes, it was rather touching, in that."

"Doesn't it seem incredible," Lillias mused, "that people who have once cared for each other should come to that? I can understand death, but I can't understand divorce—between husband and wife, I mean."

"And yet, that's where it's commonest," he suggested, without apparent sense of the joke.

"It seems to be," she agreed. "What else did they say?"

"The rest was mainly an exchange of insults."

The lovers were silent for a little space, and then she asked, "Doesn't it seem strange, that just in this supreme moment, when we are promising our lives to each other, and trying to join them in the sweetest hopes, those poor people should be so near us—in the next house, in the next room—tearing themselves apart in the darkest despair and the bitterest hate! Do you think there is anything ominous in it?"

"I don't see why there should be. While I heard them talking, last night, of course I couldn't help thinking of ourselves. But *our* love is very different, Lillias. It isn't founded on any mere personal fancy. It is rea-

Miss Bellard's Inspiration

soned and reasonable. It has been thought
out seriously and soberly from the very beginning. I was in love with the idea of you
before I saw you—with the girl who was doing the sort of thing that you were doing,
and must be the sort of girl you were. When
I saw you, I saw that I had been merely ful-
filling my destiny."

"You said that." Lillias paused from
this beginning, and then continued. "I suppose there was some other—attraction. I'm
free to say there was with me, Edmund," she
tenderly entreated him.

"Oh, there was with me, too—*afterwards*.
So much so that at times, now, I'm afraid I
forget the original motive, altogether."

"Oh, how sweetly you say it," she beamed
upon him. She started up with him, and he
was quicker than before because now they
met half-way of the table. She said, in a
matter-of-fact way, "I suppose, if we're going
for a walk, I had better get my hat."

Miss Bellard's Inspiration

"Oh, certainly, dearest. And I will get mine, too."

They laughed together at their reciprocal imbecility, and once more he was very quick; or rather they were both very quick.

VI

RS. CROMBIE went into Crombie's library to receive the stranger, whose card was coming up for her husband, an hour or so after Craybourne and Lillias had left the house. She intercepted the card, for she was just going in to see why Crombie was not getting up, even for the belated breakfast which he ordinarily made. He said, as if he needed any excuse for being lazy, that he was not feeling just like himself that morning, and he thought he would take it out in bed till luncheon. Then he should be fresher, and more equal to things. He did not say what the things were that he needed being equal to, and she did not press him for an explanation. He glanced drowsily at the card she gave him, and she descended to the library, prepared with a good conscience to say to the stranger that Mr. Crombie had begged her to see him, and was very sorry not to be well enough to come himself. She added, to a visible preoccupation of the stranger's, that she hoped she could be Mr. Crombie's substitute.

"Oh, by all means," the stranger returned, standing up during these preliminaries, and supporting what seemed an habitual lameness on the stick he held in his hand. Mrs. Crombie asked him to sit down, and she was the more civil to him in her tone because of a certain distinction in his presence. He was very well set up, and his voice was well managed, and he had the air of the world which we all prize in ourselves and others.

"I don't know why I should expect Mr. Crombie to remember me, after such a time," he said, looking down as with an habitual glance and tapping his boot with his stick, "but when I made out that it was actually he who was living here, I couldn't resist dropping over. I'm at the Saco Shore House." He lifted his head. "My name is Mevison; Mr. Crombie and I knew each other in Paris."

Mrs. Crombie started dramatically. "Not *Arthur* Mevison! Of Réné's atelier?"

"Yes."

"Why, Mr. Crombie did nothing but talk of you, after we were married, for years and years! I used to perfectly die of wonder that we never saw you; I saw all the rest of his bachelor friends, and he always said that you would be sure to turn up. But you never did. I'm so glad! I'll rush up and tell him who it is; I don't believe he really looked at your card. Why, he'll be wild!" She bolted towards the door with an agility impredicable of her bulk, but something in his look indefinitely detained her.

"No, don't disturb Crombie! I couldn't

Miss Bellard's Inspiration

wait till he's dressed—if he's still in bed. I just dropped over. We shall be at the hotel some days. Perhaps he'll look in on me. It's quite enough for the present to know that we're so near each other. Don't!"

There was such a note of pathos in his entreaty that she provisionally forbore, but as much in curiosity as in compassion, and he added, "I'm rather glad *not* to see him this morning; he'll know how to account for that, if he remembers me as well as I remember him. Do let me go, and come back again!"

"Will you come back soon? To luncheon?" she parleyed.

"Well—ah—perhaps not to luncheon—"

"I beg your pardon! Of course Mrs. Mevison is with you. I will go over and bring her back with me, and you will both stay to luncheon."

"I don't believe Mrs. Mevison—"

"Well, we will see!" Mrs. Crombie cried, in

prepotent hospitality. "I know the table at the Saco Shore, and how glad hotel-bound people are of a little home food, if you put it on the lowest ground. Have they made you comfortable as to rooms?"

"Oh, I think so. They've done their best, I dare say. Mrs. Mevison is a nervous sufferer, and sometimes the best isn't the most she could ask; but it's very well; the rooms are rather high up—"

"Now, I'll tell you what, Mr. Mevison," Mrs. Crombie broke in upon him. "We're not going to let you stay there. We are going to have you here. We have plenty of rooms that are mere aching voids at present, and it will be not only a pleasure but a mercy. This place is my doing, and Mr. Crombie misses the society we used to have at the sea-shore, and is always more or less pining for people. To have *you*, of *all* people— and Mrs. Mevison! Can't you understand?"

"Dimly," Mr. Mevison returned. "But the thing is simply impossible—"

"Not till Mrs. Mevison says so," Mrs. Crombie gayly retorted. "It will be such a surprise for Mr. Crombie. Now, I won't really take no for an answer, or at least any no but your wife's. It won't be the least disturbance to us, if that's what you mean. It will be an unmitigated blessing. Don't say another word. The thing is simply settled."

"No, my dear Mrs. Crombie, it isn't settled," he protested, with a solemnity which in another mood must have impressed her. "It can't be—"

But she took this for a polite pretence, and laughed him down, in saying, "Well, it shall be just as you wish, Mr. Mevison. Only, I suppose I may go and call upon Mrs. Mevison?"

"Mrs. Mevison will be very glad to see you," he said, gravely, and after a little more hilarious fatuity of hers and embarrassed helplessness of his, he took his leave with her promise, or her threat, that she would bring Crombie with her to call upon Mrs. Mevison.

She meant to keep the matter a secret from Crombie, and to have an agreeable mystery for him in making him go to the inn, to call with her upon some old friends of his whom she should not name; but she did not find in herself the strength for this. As soon as Mr. Mevison was out of the house, she pounded breathlessly up-stairs to Crombie, who was still drowsing, in a vain security from what was about to happen, and called out to him as soon as she opened the door, "Well, now, Archibald, who do you think has been here?"

He said, of course, that he did not know, and then she came out with "Arthur Mevison!"

He returned sleepily, sceptically, conditionally, "What Arthur Mevison?"

Miss Bellard's Inspiration

"Why, *your* Arthur Mevison that you've always told me about—Paris Réné's favorite pupil. Surely you're not going to—"

Crombie sat up in bed. "You don't mean to tell me that Arthur Mevison— I thought he was dead!"

"He isn't dead in the least. He's staying at the Saco Shore with his wife—"

"With his *wife?*"

"Yes; what is there so strange about that? Did you know her?"

"Oh no."

"What do you know about her? What have you ever heard of her?"

"Nothing definite. Only that she was a thundering fool of some sort."

"Then that accounts for it. Tell me all about her, before you go one inch further, Archibald."

"I've always told you all about her. How she broke him up as soon as she could, and made him leave off painting, and tag her round the world everywhere, and wouldn't let him live six months in any one place, and quarrelled with all his friends and enemies, and led him a dog's life, and played the devil generally."

"You never told me one word of the kind."

"Didn't I?" he returned, easily. "I thought I did."

"Not one word! And you have got me into an awful scrape."

Crombie lay down again, and pulled the coverlet to his chin, as if he could take the consequences better in that posture. "What have you done?"

"Done? I have asked them to come and stay with us. I thought it would be such a pleasant surprise for you."

"Why, you don't mean to say that she's been here in the house with him?"

"Not at all! But I've asked him, and I've said I was going over to ask her. And I shall have to do it."

"Oh, well! Very likely there's no harm done. But I thought you had your hands rather full with Lillias and her young man, and you wouldn't want any more guests just now. Besides, if *he* wants to come, very likely *she* won't. I've understood that it usually works that way with them." He meant not only the Mevisons, but all people in the like case.

"But he doesn't want to come! And I wouldn't take no for an answer. I insisted upon going and asking her."

Crombie puckered his mouth to a long, low whistle.

"And that is the sort of scrape you have got me into, my dear. How often have I told you that your habit of supposing you had spoken of things would be the ruin of us some day!"

"Oh, well," Crombie said after a moment's reflection, "perhaps it isn't so bad as I've heard. It was some talk of Minver's at

94

the club when I was down at New York last winter. He said she had spoiled the most promising career in the world. Minver seemed to want to kill her. But he's an awful tongue, Minver is. Well, it can't be helped now."

"No, it can't be helped now," Mrs. Crombie echoed. "And the sooner I make the plunge the better," she added, strenuously as to her words, but, as to her actions, with the effect of shivering on the verge. In order to gird herself up, she argued, "I said luncheon, and I suppose I ought to go at once."

"Yes," Crombie assented in great personal comfort, "I suppose you had. *I* can't."

His wife tacitly examined his moral armor for some crevice at which to pierce him with inculpation, but finding it proof against her she could only say, as she turned to sweep out of the room, "Well, for goodness' sake,

Archy, do be up to receive them if I bring them back with me!"

"Oh, that will be all right," he answered cosily from the depths of his selfish security; but by-and-by, when she called through his closed door that she was going, he stretched himself in bed with decision, and really began to push off the blanket.

Mrs. Crombie, as she issued into the irregular avenue of elms that formed the approach to her cottage from the river, saw a couple advancing towards her. In the distance they seemed united by the simple device of the man's having his arm round the woman's waist; as they came nearer, this appearance yielded to the effect of her having her hand through his arm; and by the time they were unmistakably Lillias and Craybourne, they were walking less and less closely together. "Upon my word," Mrs. Crombie said to herself, "Lillias is going it!" But to Lillias, then within hail, she called, "I'm just running over to the hotel, to see some old friends of your uncle's. I shall have to leave the house in your charge while I'm gone."

"Well, I dare say I can get Mr. Craybourne to help keep the robbers away."

"I guess you'll have to. Your *uncle* isn't up yet. It's a Mr. Mevison and his wife," she explained at random. "He used to be in Réné's atelier with your uncle, but he gave it up after he was married. She wouldn't let him. I wonder if Mr. Craybourne has met them at the hotel."

"One meets a great many people at the Saco Shore House," the young man replied, not wholly able to keep his eyes away from Lillias's waist.

"Do you suppose it could have been the people," the girl asked him, "who were inquiring about aunty's cottage?"

A look of alarm came into the dark face of

97

the young man. "It's possible. I'm sure I can't say."

"Well, you'd better, if they're the ones you heard conversing so violently at night."

Craybourne stood looking at her and wondering what she was giving him away for in that fashion. She explained indirectly. "Forewarned is forearmed, Aunt Hester. I hope it isn't the couple that Mr. Craybourne says are carrying on a running fight, over there."

"Horrors!" Mrs. Crombie said. "What does she mean?" she asked the young man.

"Really, it can't be the same. I was telling Miss Bel—Lillias—of a family jar that I had been rather obliged to overhear part of last night; but there's no reason to suppose—"

"He means there's every reason to suppose," the girl put in mischievously.

"I see," Mrs. Crombie said, "and it coincides with your uncle's view of her." She turned from Lillias to the young man. "Was it very—"

Craybourne merely looked unhappy, but Lillias easily answered for him: "They didn't throw things, as far as he could make out, but anything short of that!"

Mrs. Crombie remembered the dignity she had lost sight of in her curiosity. "I think there is some mistake. The Mr. and Mrs. Mevison I am speaking of are middle-aged people, and I have asked him to let me bring them over to stay with us. They are not very comfortable at the hotel."

"It seems to be rather full," Craybourne vaguely assented.

In the presence of a calamity on which Mrs. Crombie put so bold a face, the girl was sobered. "I've no idea they are the same people, aunty." Then she gave way again to the spirit of mischief which her happiness seemed to have awakened in her. "But if they do happen to be, it's the very contrast

99

you want, to us. If you don't get somebody of that kind into the house, I don't see how you are going to live through us. We're bad enough now, but we're going to be worse. At least, Mr. Craybourne is."

She looked teasingly from her aunt to her lover, and it seemed as if he were not able to gainsay her; as if he had no wish to do so; as if what she said was final wisdom as well as primal love. He was a sight to make another man sick, but his aspect filled Mrs. Crombie with reverence. She was not a ready or epigrammatical woman, but she had the inspiration of answering, "I should be willing to take my chances with you two alone."

"Oh, poor aunty!" the girl cried, with a laugh, in which they all senselessly joined.

Mrs. Crombie moved on towards the ferry, and the young people towards the house. She had met them midway of the avenue, and at its foot Mrs. Crombie turned and looked back towards them at its head; they were turning, too, as well as they could, and she perceived that she had lost the intermediate step towards the closer union which had been represented before by Lillias's having her hand through Craybourne's arm.

VII

MRS. MEVISON received Mrs. Crombie in her husband's presence, with the prompt and peculiar smile with which ladies know how to condone men's clumsy blunders. He was getting lamely up from his newspaper to introduce the two women, when his wife came gracefully forward with outstretched hand, saying, in a sort of tender warble, "Mrs. Crombie?" She had certainly a very winning voice, and her manner was perfection; if it had been less perfect, perhaps it might have been better.

"Arthur," she cried to her husband, "do get Mrs. Crombie a chair, and let us all sit down on the veranda here. The best part of these summer hotels is the outside, don't you think? I was sure you would come, when Arthur told me he had been to look you up, though he always keeps such things as a little surprise for me."

Mrs. Mevison was bending and smiling, and sweeping herself into a chair after Mrs. Crombie was seated, and wanting to give her a fan or take something from her, or make her have an easier seat, and ignoring her excuses for Crombie's failure to come, too, with an angelic amiability which deceived neither of them. They both knew that Mevison had said nothing to his wife about the Crombies' coming, and they understood that Mrs. Mevison was now taking it out of him for his failure to do so. He cast a certain look upon Mrs. Crombie, as if he would say: "Now, here is your chance to back out of your hospitality. I haven't said anything about it, and *you* needn't."

Mrs. Crombie was above any such meanness. "Men are so forgetful!" she joined

Mrs. Mevison in politely assuming. Then, for this would not quite do, she said, " They seem to have a passion for surprises, and are always keeping things back to spring them on you."

"Mr. Mevison," his wife said, with an arch glance at him which did not disperse the kind of darkness involving him, "likes to keep them back *without* springing them on you." She continued to look tenderly across her shoulder at him while Mrs. Crombie went on, but her jaw was set.

"Well, I hope you won't find this surprise too formidable. It's merely that I want you to come over and stay with us as long as you meant to stay at the hotel, and as much longer as we can make you. And I won't take no for answer!"

"What do you say, dearest?" Mrs. Mevison asked, with melting meekness, in referring the question to her husband. Then she referred his attitude ironically to Mrs. Crombie. " You see what a tyrant I have! I can't say my soul's my own in these matters!" she concluded gayly.

Mevison ignored her in replying to Mrs. Crombie: "I really couldn't think of our crowding in upon you. We're very comfortable here, though that has nothing to do with it; and it wouldn't be fair to sacrifice you to my old friendship with Crombie—"

Mrs. Crombie would have lifted her voice in protest; she had indeed got it incoherently up, when Mrs. Mevison cut in under it with a warble of the sweetest caressingness: " Now, dearest! I *must, just for once*, put in my little plea! I don't think it at all nice for you to say it's quite comfortable here as a reason for refusing Mrs. Crombie's kindness—"

"I admitted something like that," he growled, without looking at her.

She patted the air towards him with a small, glittering, jewelled hand. "Now, now, now! You know I'm not criticising you,

love. I simply can't have Mrs. Crombie
misunderstand you. I must have her know
that it's merely your delicacy, and that you're
dying to be with your old friend, for those
long, late talks that men can have only when
they've risen from the same table and are going to bed under the same roof. You must
own, now, that I couldn't keep you from
rushing over to Mr. Crombie's as soon as you
had breakfast this morning, and that you're
just dying to accept Mrs. Crombie's invita-
tion." She turned vividly to Mrs. Crombie.
" That's the true version, Mrs. Crombie, and
I'm going to accept for him." She warbled
down the disclaimer that he tried to make.
" We will be in good time for luncheon—half-
past one? No, one!—and I will see to having our things sent over later in the day; you
needn't trouble about them! And Mr. Mevison won't, either! He's all a man when it
comes to packing, though he *doesn't* always
have the courage of his preferences."

Miss Bellard's Inspiration

She laughed to Mrs. Crombie at the discomfiture and confusion in his face, and Mrs. Crombie, presently getting up to go, with some polite fatuities about being so glad they could come, and all that, Mrs. Mevison rose too, of course, and went over to her husband where he had risen, and grouped herself affectionately with him, laying her pretty hand on his arm, which, while Mrs. Crombie still admired, twitched itself from her as with a nervous impatience.

They followed Mrs. Crombie down to the foot of the veranda stairs in her going, and there repeated their leave of her. Then Mrs. Mevison tripped girlishly up the stairs, and with a gay cry of laughter ran back into the hotel before her husband.

Mrs. Crombie walked very soberly home, and, as the sum of her reflections, said to her husband, whom she met in the avenue, going over at last to do the decencies in calling upon his friend: "Well, Archibald, I can't make

her out, and I don't believe you can. But
you needn't go, now. They've accepted, or
she has, and they'll be to lunch. I'm afraid
we're in for something awful."

He turned with her. "Why, what makes
you think so?"

"Well, she may be thundering, but she's
no fool."

"What makes you think that?"

"I couldn't begin to tell you. We'd better
wait and see if you can see. I don't want
to prejudice you against her."

"Apparently not."

"But this I *will* say: she's either the most
consummate actress, or the fondest wife, or
the most perfect little fiend that I ever did
see."

"Come! That's something like impartial
treatment. She couldn't be all three?"

"She might. But didn't you always tell
me that Mevison was a man of the greatest
courage?"

Miss Bellard's Inspiration

"He was the cock of the atelier. Was going to fight a duel with one of the Frenchmen, and cowed the fellow out by his choice of revolvers for weapons. He confessed that he couldn't have hit the side of a barn, afterwards."

"That is what I always understood. Well!"

"Do you mean that Mrs. Mevison has taken the pluck out of him?"

"Not that. But she has bewildered him. She does what she pleases with him, because he can't follow her. Archibald, I never saw a man that I liked so much!—except you, of course!"

"Thank you. I dare say he has his faults. He used to have them; perhaps Mrs. Mevison has reformed him. But I notice that a woman always attributes the fault in these cases to the wife, unless the case happens to be her own. What did you see or hear that made you suspect Mrs. Mevison of not being a saint upon earth?"

"Well, everything that I heard was in her favor. He seemed very sulky, though he was perfectly polite to me; and perhaps I only fancied what I saw."

"What was it?"

"She laid her hand on his arm, when we all got up, and smoothed it, and suddenly he twitched away, as if something had stung him."

"You mean, she pinched him?"

"I can't be sure that she did."

"And it's that sort of calamity you've asked into our house! Perhaps it would have been as well to wait and make Mrs. Mevison's acquaintance."

"I did it for your sake. I thought you would like to have your old friend here."

"I know you did, and I don't blame you. Well, it will be rather interesting. It will be a show. Poor old Mevison!"

"Yes, my heart aches for him. Archibald,

do you suppose there is much of that kind of misery in the world?"

"Lots."

"Then marriage *is* a failure!"

"In those instances. It all comes from their expecting too much of it. I still incline to the theory that Mrs. Mevison is a thundering fool. Well, it will be a good object-lesson for Lillias and her love. It will teach them to go slow in their demands upon each other. I always heard that the Mevisons were furiously in love; and she seems to be in love yet."

"Do you call pinching love?"

"It's one form of it. It's the hating and hurting form."

"Now, Archibald, you are beginning to be disgusting again."

VIII

MRS. MEVISON made the luncheon go off so nicely that Crombie, at least, began to think his wife's eyes must have deceived her, and there could have been no pinching or baffling or bewildering on the part of such a woman as she showed herself. She deferred to Mevison in everything; when there was nothing to defer to him in, she invented things. She made Crombie tell her all about Mevison's life and his in Réné's atelier; she confessed that she was jealous of everybody who had known her husband before she had, and she said that if Réné had taken girl pupils, she did not know what she should do, so intimately as art students were thrown together.

"Oh, but he did," Crombie said.

"He *did?* Why, dearest," she turned to her husband, "didn't you always tell me that Réné didn't take girl pupils?"

"No," Mevison answered, briefly.

"How very strange! I must have dreamed it. I knew that I couldn't bear it if it was so, and so I simply dreamed it wasn't."

She took the able-minded Lillias and her lover into her especial favor, though she extended her favor to the whole household, and there was not a servant whom she came in contact with whose heart she did not make it her business to win. Mrs. Crombie had acquainted her at once with the absorbing psychological situation which Lillias and Craybourne embodied, and extracted from her a warble that was also a crow of sympathetic exultation. "Oh, how perfectly *dear!* It's just as if it had been planned for *us.* Lovers! Arthur and I have never ceased to be lovers. And to think that it should be that delightful young Englishman who has been sitting at our table at the inn! I *must* tell Arthur? May I?"

She frankly possessed herself of Craybourne at once, and by her brave unconsciousness defied him beyond his powers to think evil of anything he had seen of her; as to what he had heard he began to doubt that too. While she captured Craybourne with one hand, she playfully threatened Lillias with the other. "Don't you turn those pretty eyes of yours on my husband, Miss Bellard! I won't have it! The poor fellow couldn't stand their fire a half-minute if I were not here; or if Mr. Craybourne wasn't; *he'll* help me save him."

She treated Lillias alternately as a chit and as a veteran worldling who knew it all, and whom nothing need be kept from. During the whole of the first day she pretended that the girl was Crombie's niece, and insinuated a subtile and delicate compassion for Mrs. Crombie in having the burden of her affair in the house, together with the responsibility. When she consented to understand that Lillias was the daughter of Mrs. Crombie's sister, nothing could exceed the pleasure she had in Crombie's good nature and her sympathy with Mrs. Crombie's sense of it. One did so hate to ask things of one's husband! She had made it a principle to die before letting Arthur do anything for her that she could possibly help. She was struck with fresh wonder at Lillias: her remarkable beauty, which was so different from the ordinary beauty; her grace, which was as wholly her own as if she had invented the idea of grace; her brilliancy, which was so unlike the brilliancy of girls who were thought brilliant in the usual acceptation of the term. She said that Mrs. Crombie must tell her all about Lillias, and she made her tell her at least all she wished to know of the girl's strange career, her odd notions of independence, how and where she met Mr. Craybourne, and what his credentials were, and how utterly devoted they were to each other. She said that very few Americans would have fallen in love with a girl under such very peculiar circumstances; it was only an Englishman who could do it, and everybody that knew said that Englishmen made the best of lovers and the worst of husbands.

By this time Crombie wanted to put her out of the house, to throw her into the Saco; and his fury gratified Mrs. Crombie as a generous tribute to her niece. "I don't like her any more than you do, Archibald," she said, "but she interests me, and you needn't feel anxious about Lillias. She can be trusted to take care of herself, when she gets round to it, as the country people say. It's very sweet of you to think of her, but you mustn't, dearest, though I appreciate it. Everything is going swimmingly. I've given you and Mr. Mevison a chance to bring up your arrears of talk, and I don't believe they'll stay long. I noticed this morning when I was in her room that she had hardly hung up a thing; there's one of her trunks that she hasn't even unlocked. So you needn't worry, you poor thing!"

She put her hand on the gloved hand of Crombie, in which he held the reins of the horse he was driving on an excursion stolen from their guests. She had done her duty in proposing a buckboard that they could all six have driven in; when Lillias declined that, and urged Mr. Craybourne to go, Mrs. Crombie devolved upon a carryall for four, but so forbiddingly that Mrs. Mevison laughed at the notion of Mevison and herself foisting themselves upon their hosts for the only relief they could have from their hospitalities. She said she would make Arthur take her a walk; it was a pity his lameness would not let him do any mountain-climbing; the mountain-climbing there must be so easy.

Miss Bellard's Inspiration

She must get Mr. Craybourne and Lillias to take her with them some time; she doted on mountain-climbing.

Lillias said, gravely, perhaps Mr. Craybourne would take her now; she would stay and see that Mr. Mevison came to no harm while they were gone; but after an infinitesimal moment in which Craybourne manifested a perdurable resolution not to take Mrs. Mevison mountain-climbing, she warbled back, Oh no! She could never leave Mr. Mevison alone while she was enjoying herself; and she warned Lillias against the insidious effect of giving way to the emotions, which was always in danger of becoming such a fixed habit that you had no peace of your life.

For these reasons the Crombies found themselves driving alone, and quit of the sight of all their guests until, on the home-stretch, they arrived at a mowing-piece not far from their cottage, but secluded from the sight of it. There they saw the Mevisons walking together at the farther side of the meadow, and well beyond hearing of their wheels. He had his hands folded on his stick behind him, and was limping along between the hay-cocks which dotted the smoothly cropped stubble, while she playfully came and went, dropping after him, and then passing ahead of him, apparently saying something to him, and either laughing or crying, they could not make out which. Suddenly, she gave a scream of unmistakable rage, with a sort of rush at him; then he was gripping her wrists and vividly expostulating with her.

"Oh, Archibald!" Mrs. Crombie wailed; "Do you, can you, believe she meant to—"

"Not a doubt of it!" In his transport, Crombie gave a cut of the whip to the horse, which, after a moment of astonishment at treatment so unprecedented, bolted into a short trot that carried them temporarily

9

past the belligerents. As soon as the horse slowed up, Crombie looked back round the side of his buggy.

"Can you see them?" his wife palpitated.

"Yes, and she's walking beside him as peaceably as a lamb. Well, upon my soul, if she isn't waving her handkerchief to me!"

"Then," his wife commanded, "take off your hat and bow, so that she'll think we haven't seen them. Smile!"

"Not much!" Crombie said, grimly, without doing either, and this forced his wife, at great personal inconvenience, to get up and wave her handkerchief over the top of the buggy.

At dinner, Mrs. Mevison came radiantly down, warbling out as she took her place rather belatedly, "Such a game of romps as Arthur and I had in your hay-field, Mr. Crombie! You wouldn't think, with his lameness, how quick he is. I hope we didn't spoil the hay."

"Oh," Crombie said, "if you were having fun, I don't mind the hay."

IX

HE Crombies decided that in the interest of young love they would keep what they had seen in the mowing-piece from Lillias and Craybourne. It was not that the girl was so ignorant of life as not to know that husbands and wives have their little tiffs, but a convention of the kind that forbids elders recognizing the knowledge of children concerning all sorts of things constrained them to the pretence that marriage is an indefinite continuation of love's young dream. Craybourne, indeed, might be supposed acquainted with darkling things about life outside of matrimony, but he could not decently be imagined privy to the fact that people joined in wedlock ever chafed in their bonds.

Miss Bellard's Inspiration

Lillias, in her preparation for the stage, must have come so well in sight of the theatre as to have learned that there were such things as quarrels and separations among actors; but unless she recurred to her experience with her own father and mother she must have believed that such casualties were incidents solely of the histrionic temperament and profession. In spite of her frank recognition to her aunt of the situation which Craybourne had noted at the hotel, and had apparently talked over with her, the Crombies felt sacredly bound not to let her suspect it.

Crombie felt himself the more strictly enjoined to reticence from the girl by the enlargement of his own knowledge a few nights later. It came in the form of a confidence from Mevison as they sat smoking late on the veranda, watching the planets over the fiery points of their cigars and fighting the occasional mosquitoes which came just often enough to bear Crombie out in saying that they had no mosquitoes to speak of. It began with the voluntary confession that Mevison made of his not having slept very well the night before.

"What was the matter?" Crombie grunted comfortably through his smoke. "Bed bad?"

"No, the fault was with the man in it. I've got the trick of not sleeping very well."

"I remember when you couldn't be kept awake."

"Oh," Mevison laughed, forlornly, "I didn't have the right one to keep me awake, then." He piteously burst out: "For God's sake, Crombie, don't pretend you don't see how it is with my wife and me!"

"No, I won't, Mevison," his friend returned, kindly. "Do you want me to ask you what the trouble is?"

"Oh, the usual trouble: incompatibility. We're fighting to a separation. I didn't want it to go to the extreme—to a divorce; but

Miss Bellard's Inspiration

I'm resigned to that now, because I see we are impossible to each other. I've seen it for years; I've seen it from the first."

"Yes," Crombie said, feeling that Mevison wished to be prompted.

"It isn't that we don't love each other, or that we haven't. We've always loved each other too much. I won't brag of my part, but I know that when she's been the most impossible she's been the most devoted to me. She cared for me so entirely that she could not bear that anybody—no! any *thing* —else should have the least part of me. You used to believe I could paint? Or could have painted if I had kept on?"

"You could have been a *great* painter."

"Perhaps. But she broke it up. It wasn't merely that the models drove her mad. I could excuse her for that; I think it's pretty hard for an artist's wife to bear, and I've come to think it's an unhallowed thing for a man to keep looking at a woman's nakedness and putting her beauty down in color. But when I left off working from models, and took to *chicquing* it—did the ideal business—it was just as bad. Then I found out that it was the painting itself which she felt between us. If there had been a necessity for my working, if there had been poverty, I might have gone on; I should have had to. But there was money, plenty of it— hers. So I left off, for peace' sake, thinking I could begin again some time; and we began to drift. We've been round the world half a dozen times; we've lived in twenty coun- tries; but we always had ourselves with us. She wasn't jealous, or at least not of women more than of men. But she felt that I was all hers, and that she had a right to every atom, every instant of me. If I made a friend, she broke up the friendship. Not in any public way—I must say she always managed skilfully at first, though of late she's been growing reckless. But it was slavery."

Miss Bellard's Inspiration

"I see," Crombie assented, but very gingerly, so as not to interrupt Mevison.

"Still," he went on, "I was not the only sufferer. Slavery was always worse for the owner than the slave. I know it hurt her worse than it hurt me; that it was anguish for her to make me miserable, as she had to do, because she loved me, in her way so much. It caused her pain and shame and sorrow twice as much as it caused me. She knew that she spoiled my life, and that whether I was aware of it or not, at the bottom of my soul I longed to be rid of her; to break my chain, to pull my neck out of the halter at any cost. The conviction grew upon her, and goaded her, till she had to accuse me of it. I knew the truth first from her; and the time came when I couldn't deny it; though I denied it at first a thousand times, I had to own it at last. That made things intolerable. What she could bear, so long as I denied it, she could not bear when I owned it, though she had divined it herself, and brought me to the sense of it. What is the use of making a short story long? She sees as well as I do that we must part; but it is her helpless fate to torment me more and more into what if we could we would both avoid."

"I think I can understand," Crombie said, modestly enough, for subtleties like these were not his strong point. He had a notion of suggesting that something might be done, but upon the whole he felt that nothing had better be done, even if it could, and that the most that could be hoped or asked for these miserable people was a separation for time, if not for eternity.

"I don't mean to say," Mevison continued, getting up and throwing the stump of his cigar over the veranda rail, "that I haven't been to blame. But the accurate way of putting it would be to say that neither of us is to blame. We were simply born not to be mated, and we have been mated. That's all."

Crombie had his own opinion as to the totality. In his heart he did not the least blame his friend, and he did blame Mrs. Mevison. He was in the presence of his friend's quivering anguish, his humiliation and despair, and he did not believe the woman who caused it could share it in the measure that Mevison believed. He would have liked to say something of the sort, but besides being a little insecure of his phrasing, he was uncertain how Mevison might take it. The next thing was to sympathize with Mevison about his not sleeping. "Did you ever try Scotch whiskey for your insomnia? I find that sets *me* off about as quick as anything."

"I don't know," Mevison hesitated. "I think I can manage without, to-night, I'm so dead tired. The worst of it is that if the whiskey fails it leaves you twice as rotten as if you had simply lain awake without it. Still!"

"Better try it," Crombie urged. "It can't fail if you take enough of it." They went in-doors and Crombie got a bottle down from one of the book-shelves in his library, where it seemed to be doing duty as literature. He found a tumbler on the shelf, and he went out to the dining-room for some water and sugar. Mevison refused the sugar, and Crombie said, "You don't want to put in too much water, either." Mevison put in so little as to leave the whiskey he drank off almost neat. "There," Crombie said, " I guess that will fetch you." He poured some water into a tumbler, and handed it to Mevison with the bottle of whiskey. "Better take it up with you. If the first dose don't do the business, the second will, sure."

Mevison obeyed him, and crept slowly up the stairs while Crombie stayed to put out the lights and follow him with a candle.

Miss Bellard's Inspiration

"Give me something to read," he whispered on the upper landing. "Something good and dull. I find that sets me off at times."

"Novel?" Crombie suggested.

"No; the cheapest story interests me too much. Haven't you got some sort of travels—old sort?"

Crombie found on a hanging shelf in the hall a volume which Mevison said would do, and they bade each other good-night. Everybody else, plainly, was asleep, and Crombie, unused as he was to such psychological reflections, felt a fine conjecture penetrate him as to the dreams of the several people slumbering in their several rooms. He dismissed his wife's briefly, because for one thing she would be sure to tell them to him when she woke; but he hung upon those of Lillias Bellard, whose chamber was on one side of Mevison's room, with a doorless wall between, and those of Mrs. Mevison, whose room, on the other side, opened into her husband's.

Miss Bellard's Inspiration

It occurred to Crombie that the girl's visions probably concerned a radiant future, and the woman's a radiant past, and that this state was in both cases the same. He did not know whether the hope of it or the despair of it was the worse, and, having no one there to help him guess, he gave it up, as if it were a conundrum, and opened his own door, across the hall from those of his three guests, and let himself in very softly, so as not to disturb his wife, who slept in the room next his.

X

MRS. MEVISON came down in the morning in a youthful freshness so alien to her years, though these were not very many, that every one noted it and was surprised: every one but poor Mr. Mevison, as she called him in reporting that he had had a bad night, and she had left him trying to catch a little beauty-nap. They must not wait breakfast for him; he would be all the better-looking for being allowed to take his chances later. She noted with explicit pleasure that they had not waited for her. She liked that English way of breakfasting catch-as-catch-can; perhaps that was not just the phrase. "I'm afraid your whiskey was a failure, Mr. Crombie," she sweetly turned upon the host, "though Mr. Mevison gave it a fair trial, I should say, from the looks of the bottle!"

Crombie was driven to the mistake of excusing himself. "There wasn't much in the bottle when he took it."

"There certainly wasn't much when he left it!" she crowed back. "There's a little remedy of mine that I give him, when I find out he's not been sleeping, that *never* fails. But the difficulty is to find out. Men are so odd! I'm the last to know such a thing; I suppose he thinks it will worry me. I shall give *you* some, Mr. Crombie, and the next time he complains to you I want you to offer it instead of the whiskey—as if it were your own invention. Won't that be *good!*"

She bade them please not stay at table with her, and Crombie went into his library, while Mrs. Crombie went to interview the cook about luncheon and dinner. Lillias had al-

ready slipped away and found Craybourne
mysteriously arrived on the veranda, where
he must have been in telepathic communion
with her for some minutes before she left the
table. She sat down on the upper tread of
the stairs leading to the lawn at the side
of the house, and he on a tread lower,
which brought his head on a level with hers.
She leaned forward with her elbows on her
knees, her hands pressed together, and her
face slanted towards his in a pose favorable
to the confidences they at once began ex-
changing.

"I never knew," he said, "that your eyes
were so very blue."

"Nor I that yours were so very black.
But mine are really bluish green. What are
yours, really?"

"Blackish green, I suppose." He took
one of her hands from the other and examined it carefully, without and within, and
then restored it to her.

10

"Will it do?" she asked. "Is it the rose-leaf pattern?"

"It's exquisite," he sighed. "It's the prime agent of your grace. I remember it in the air, at your lectures out there; no more like a 'gesture' than the movement of a bough in the wind or the sweep of a bird's wing."

"Now, that is true poetry," Lillias tenderly mocked. "What do you think of my looks generally, this morning?"

"Generally?"

"Yes; I flattered myself that I looked something like a faded flower."

"You look like the red, red rose that's newly something in June."

"Tea, tea rose, you *mean*. But one gets credit for nothing!" she sighed. "I hardly slept last night."

"Poor girl! What happened?"

"Dreadful things, grewsome things, things to take the heart out of one." She looked round over her shoulder, and saw Mrs. Mevison advance from the doorway to the rail of the veranda, on which she leaned while examining the sky. She knew that Mrs. Mevison had seen her look round, but they both pretended unconsciousness; and Mrs. Mevison went in-doors. Then Lillias said, "I had bad dreams."

"My bad dreams come from something I've eaten; but I know that yours must be purely psychological. What were they about?" he asked.

"I hate to tell you. About a lovers' quarrel"—she looked again—"a married lovers' quarrel." She paused and then added, abruptly, "I dreamed that a woman came into her husband's room, and woke him out of his sleep, and began accusing and upbraiding him. He groaned, and told her it was the first sleep he had had for nights, and implored her to go away. Then he began to threaten, and she to laugh— Oh, Edmund, it was terrible!"

The tears came, and she stretched her
hands to him as for help. When he offered to take them she pulled them back.
"No, no! I may be just so, sometime; and
you—"

The soft plapping of a woman's footfall
made itself heard, and, with another glance
over her shoulder, Lillias saw Mrs. Mevison
prowling to and fro at the farther end of the
veranda, and busying herself with putting in
place some fallen trailers of honeysuckle.
Lillias clutched her lover's hand and pulled
him away down over the lawn into the avenue leading to the river. There she bathed
her eyes with water which he scooped up
and held in his joined hands for her. Then,
seated on a grassy bank, above a sunny
ripple of the stream, they continued their
study of the lamentable case that had fallen
in their way, and tried to divine the lesson
of it for themselves.

"There can't be any doubt," she said,

"about her loving him. A woman couldn't do such things to a man she was indifferent to, or one that she simply hated. She loves him, I can see it in every look she gives him; and what do you suppose is the trouble?"

"Perhaps," he suggested, "he doesn't love her, and she knows it."

"No, that can't be it. If he didn't love her he would have left her long ago. He does love her; you mustn't think he doesn't."

"Dearest, I won't if you say so."

"No, not because I say so, but because it isn't true."

"Then because it isn't true."

"That is something like." She drooped a little nearer, so that their shoulders touched. "Where was I?"

"They are cruel because they are kind."

"Something of that sort. But you see, now, that love in itself isn't enough to keep people friends?"

"Do you mean that it has to be mixed with a little reason?"

"With a good deal of reason."

"Well, you shall supply the reason and I will supply the love. I'll tell you what I think the trouble is: Mrs. Mevison is a fool. I thought so the first time I saw her."

"Then she's a fool by her woman's nature, as much as by her own."

"Oh, I don't blame her for being a fool, any more than I praise you for being a sage. She wants to exact everything from her husband because she would like to give him everything—if she could."

"That doesn't sound very logical."

"It's as logical as it can be under the circumstances."

They both laughed at this, more and more fondly, and she said, "Well, then, what we have got to do is to love each other less and less."

"Something like that," he consented, and

they began throwing little sticks into the stream and watching them drift off together over the ripple.

They named them after themselves, and she said, "Now Edmund is chasing Lillias!"

"No, it's Lillias that's chasing Edmund!" he retorted.

They sauntered back to the house buoyant from their nonsense, with renewed hope and faith in themselves, and Mrs. Mevison met them at the veranda steps. Mevison was sitting there, and she called gayly, as if for him to hear: "Ah, I saw you escaping me! I wanted to follow you and eavesdrop your billing and cooing. All the world loves a lover, they say, you know, and I'm hungry for a taste of your happiness. Yes, I would eavesdrop, if I could. *Fair exchange is no robbery, is it, Miss Bellard?* What do you call each other now? You won't always call each other sweet names, but you'll always mean sweetness by any name. You mustn't

141

be astonished at the change, Miss Bellard. Why, the first time Mr. Mevison said to me, 'Stubborn little fool!' I hardly knew where to look; but I soon found out that it meant the same as ducky or dovey. Didn't it, ducky-dovey?"

She went up to Mevison, sitting gloomily tilted back in his chair, and from behind him clapped her hands on his cheeks and pressed her own cheek down on his head. When she released him, he flung his arms wildly about in the effort to recover his balance. Craybourne and Lillias ran too late to catch him from falling. Mrs. Mevison stopped herself in a shriek of laughter.

"Oh, what a shame! Do forgive me, Arthur!"

She lent her aid with the others; but Lillias saw him pushing his wife's hands away, when he could, with looks of deadly rage.

"I'm afraid," he said to Lillias, when he

142

had got back to his pose, " that I was rather ridiculous."

"Oh, no one *thought* of such a thing, Arthur," his wife said, with indignant tenderness.

"I'm so glad we were in time, Mr. Mevison," the girl said.

"You're all right now?" Craybourne asked.

With a little more polite parley the lovers got themselves away, Craybourne declaring that he must go back to the hotel. Mrs. Mevison remained superfluously putting her husband in shape, and brushing specks of imaginary dust from his clothes, and compassionately cooing over him.

Lillias went down the avenue with Craybourne to the ferry, and then trailed slowly back over the stubble, with her head down. When she lifted it she saw Mrs. Mevison sweeping swiftly towards her.

"Just one moment, Miss Bellard!" Mrs. Mevison called to her. The voice was gay,

and even arch, but there was a note of battle
in it, which no woman could have mistaken,
though a man might have been deceived.
When she came up to the girl, who was staring fearlessly at her, she broke out in tones
thick with fury: "Don't think I don't know
that you *heard*, last night. I don't say you
listened!"

"*No*, Mrs. Mevison," Lillias said, rather
dreadfully.

The woman tossed her head. "If you *had*
listened, you might have heard the good of
yourself that listeners always hear. It is
you, *you* that have added the last straw!
Do you suppose I don't know that from the
first moment my husband entered that
house you were making a set at him? Do
you suppose I can't see that your engage-
ment to that wretched cockney is a mere
blind, and that you're waiting till my husband and I are separated to transfer your
easy affections to him? Do you imagine I

couldn't feel the flirt-nature in you as soon as I came near you? Arthur and I might still have made it up; he was getting to see the trouble from my point of view, but when you came in between us—" She choked with her rage, and suddenly she changed from accusation to imploring. "*Leave* him to me, Miss Bellard, and it will all come right! I didn't intend to push him over just now, but when I saw how it shocked you, with your goody-goody pretences, I laughed, and I was glad I did it. But now, now I would give anything— I take it all back about you! Yes, I do. And I beg your pardon! I don't accuse you of anything. It is *his* fault, all his fault; and if you will only say that you will not encourage him—"

At this point Lillias did a wrong thing, but it may be contended that she was rather sorely tried. "Get away!" she said, with a contempt past description, and she advanced upon Mrs. Mevison as if she would tread her down. The other had no alternative but to slip aside.

"Don't take it so!" she besought the pitiless girl. "I know that you love Mr. Craybourne. I take back calling him a cockney. He isn't. He's fine and good. Any one can see it. And you are going to have in him what I have lost in my husband! That ought to make you a little lenient. It ought, oughtn't it? See how I humble myself to you! I hope you may never, never have to humble yourself to another woman as I am doing to you. *We* began as sweetly as you are beginning now. There was nothing I wouldn't do for him, or he for me. There never were people so devoted. And it has come to this with us! We are going to part, unless—unless you can show him that you don't care for him. I know you don't, but he thinks you do! If he knew you didn't, he would be reconciled to me, and we could be happy again. My life is wrapped up in him. Oh, if you won't have pity on me, have pity on yourself! You can't expect to be happy in your marriage if you break up mine. Give me back my husband—no, give him back to himself, his better self! If you don't, my misery will be upon you; it will bring you to judgment."

Lillias strode relentlessly on in silent scorn of the frantic woman, who pursued her at last with a long-drawn, heart-broken, heart-breaking "Oh!"

XI

A T luncheon Mrs. Mevison was of a calm that betrayed no signs of the morning's tempests. Lillias and she observed a truce that had the effect of a peace, unbroken by any hostile experience, and in the absence of Craybourne, who had apparently not found himself equal to further eventualities, Mrs. Mevison seemed less exasperated by the sense of the happiness so near and yet so far from her. She was very sweet and gentle with every one, from the waitress to Mevison, so that Crombie could scarcely credit his old friend when Mevison said, in the stroll which he took at Crombie's side a few hours before dinner, "Well, it has been amicably arranged with Mrs. Mevison."

"What do you mean?"

"We are going to part—friends."

"Has it really come to that? I was in hopes, seeing you so pleasant together at luncheon—"

Mevison shook his head sadly. "All women like to put a good face on things, and Mrs. Mevison above all other women. After we had agreed to separate peaceably, it was an easy matter to agree upon behaving ourselves decently during the brief remnant of our union. She feels, as I do, that we owe that much to you and Mrs. Crombie, if not to each other." To Crombie's vast astonishment he added, "She isn't unreasonable; you mustn't think that; and you mustn't think that in this business the fault has been altogether on her side, as I believe I told you before. I don't pretend that I'm not a trying man to live with at times. Certainly I'm trying to such a woman as Clarice. And in our rows I do my full share of the nagging. I've got a nasty temper of my own, and I give her as good as she sends, though I know all the time how much worse I'm hurting her than she is hurting me. It isn't out of any wickedness she does it; I can't make any one else understand. My God! how vulgar it all is! But it's coming to an end, quickly and quietly."

Through all this Crombie had a fuzzy notion that he was ill-used, or if not he, then Mrs. Crombie. She had asked these people into the house to do him a pleasure through her hospitality to his old friend, and now, confound them, they were abusing her hospitality with their infernal jangling, and they were going to set the seal to the outrage by breaking up under his roof. It was like having a double suicide on one's premises. It was violating the sanctities of a Christian home. It was a species of sacrilege; it was a scandal. People would say — there was no saying what people would *not* say, if

Miss Bellard's Inspiration

Mevison and his wife had this sort of burst-up on the place, with the subsequent proceedings for divorce. Mrs. Crombie and he might be dragged into the trial as witnesses. Lillias might; Craybourne might. He kept his injury out of his voice as well as he could in asking, "Do you mean that you are going to separate now, right off the handle?"

"We shall not even leave your house together, if you will allow me to leave her behind me for an hour or two. I expect to take the train for Quebec, and she will take the Boston express when it comes along. It's all arranged. We were packed in view of this possibility, this moral certainty, before we came to you."

"Well, see here, Mevison," Crombie said, with a knotted brow of extreme perplexity, "I hope it won't seem unreasonable to you if I ask you whether you can't hold up a little."

"How hold up?"

Miss Bellard's Inspiration

The two men paused in their ramble and stood facing each other.

"Hold up till you get away. Go off together, and separate at the Junction." The word dimly suggested something different to Crombie, but he ignored its suggestion; or, rather, he postponed it to its possible effect upon Mevison when he got to the Junction. "This thing is going to make a lot of talk. It's going to get into the papers; such things always do, nowadays. There'll be a raft of reporters round. My house will be snapshotted, and my wife's photograph and mine and Lillias's and Craybourne's will be grouped round yours and Mrs. Mevison's, with bits of the Saco Valley scenery, in the Sunday editions. You see?"

Mevison's jaw fell. "I see," he admitted, in a kind of dismay.

Crombie had made his point, and he started on, with Mevison limping at his side. "I hope, old fellow, you feel that I've been with you in this deplorable business, first, last, and all the time. It's very well for you to blame yourself; it's handsome, and manly, and generous, and chivalrous, and all that rot, but unless you've changed most infernally from the fellow I used to know at Réné's—"

"I have, Crombie," Mevison sadly responded. "Marriage changes a man; or, rather, it finds him out. I've been to blame; but all that's too late now."

"I'm not advocating your remaining together. It's probably best for both of you that you should separate. It seems to me that it's come to that—for a while at least. But, Mevison, don't do it here! It will break Mrs. Crombie up awfully."

Mevison laughed miserably. "It will break Mrs. Mevison up, too."

"Yes, I suppose it will. But, you see, Mrs. Crombie isn't in it as Mrs. Mevison is."

"No."

"She's tried to act nicely in the whole

business, Mrs. Crombie has; but it's killing her by inches." When Crombie made use of this image, he could not help making the reflection that Mevison might think there were a good many inches of Mrs. Crombie to kill, and that her vitality would hold out a long while in the process. He made haste to add, "Of course, I beg your pardon. But what I'm getting at is the idea of making this business as easy for Mrs. Crombie as possible. Now, why can't you two go off together and separate at the Junction? Why can't you put that idea before Mrs. Mevison? She might take to it."

Mevison frowned, in a recurrence of the disgust for his wife which Crombie's championship of himself had momentarily dissipated. "Yes, she might consent, if it were not for her cursed histrionics. She consented to my leaving her in your house, I believe, as much for the dramatic effect as anything—"

"But, don't you see? It will be a great

Miss Bellard's Inspiration

deal more dramatic for you to part at the Junction. The up-train and the down-train meet there; you get aboard one and she gets aboard the other, and that ends it."

Crombie's voice rose in a cheerfulness, as he urged his point, which it had not expressed before. But Mevison apparently did not share his gay expectation. "There's no telling how she will take the idea. I'm afraid it will lead to a review of the whole case. But I will try it with her. It is certainly your due in the matter, and Mrs. Crombie's due. I hope, Crombie, you understand how very grateful I feel towards you both?"

"Oh, that's all right, Mevison."

They dismissed the matter, from their talk, at least, and finished their stroll in such remoteness from it that Crombie was able to gather some wild sweetbrier roses and bring them home. Mrs. Mevison admired them so much when he arrived with them on the veranda where she was sitting with his wife that he gave them to her, bidding her be careful not to scratch herself.

"Oh, I know how to manage," she said. "Give me your handkerchief, Arthur," and when he held it out to her she put it round the thorny stems, and said, with a triumphant smile up into Crombie's face, "There!"

It was all very lurid to Crombie. With his privity to the impending tragedy he felt like a fiend, and in this comedy he was playing with the victim-villain of the tragedy he felt like a fool.

He was still of no very determinate conviction with respect to himself at large, when, after the women had left them that night, and Mevison and he sat over their cigars on the veranda and absently marked the Big Dipper filling its bowl with the clear night above the Presidential Range, Mevison said, in a low voice, "Well, it's all right."

"You suggested my idea to Mrs. Mevison?"

"Yes, and she took to the notion of the

Junction instantly. It satisfied the curious kind of poetry that Clarice has in her."

Crombie thought it a very curious kind of poetry, but he thought it best not to say so, and Mevison went on.

"I gave her some inkling of how you felt, and she instantly entered into your feeling. Clarice is a very reasonable woman in those things. She is very intelligent."

Mevison heaved a long, low sigh, with which he exhaled a volume of smoke, whitening in the clear, chill night air.

"Well, then," Crombie said, "if it's all settled, I hope you'll get a good night's rest, and start fresh in the morning." This was not quite what he would have wished to say, but he let it go.

"No doubt about that," Mevison returned. "As I haven't slept for several nights past, I should be pretty sure of sleeping to-night even if I didn't feel so strangely at peace. I suppose it's the peace of exhaustion.

I suppose Clarice feels the same, poor woman!"

"Better take the whiskey up with you," Crombie said, as they rose from their tobacco at last.

"No, I'm all right without, don't be afraid. Besides, Clarice has given me some sleep-medicine of hers that she finds never fails."

XII

CROMBIE also felt something of that peace from exhaustion of which Mevison had all but boasted, as he entered his room very carefully, so as not to waken Mrs. Crombie, whom he imagined asleep beyond the door opening into her own room. He was surprised to have her look in at him, as if she had been waiting up for him. But he said, as if he had expected it:

"Well, you know they're going, in the morning?"

"Yes, she told me."

"And they're going to separate, too."

"Separate!"

"You must have seen it was coming to that. I had it out with Mevison this afternoon when we were walking; but I didn't mean to tell you till they were out of the house. They meant to separate before they left us, he taking the up-train and she the down-train, an hour later. But I told him that it wouldn't do; that it would make talk about us, and bring us into their row in all sorts of ways."

"That was very thoughtful of you, Archibald."

"He saw the point, too. I made him promise that they would decently leave the house together, and leave the Saco Shore station together, and do their confounded separating at the Junction."

Crombie ended in an exasperation, in which he lifted his voice, out of the whisper they had been using, into a thick barytone.

"'Sh!" she hissed. "Don't speak so loud! You've done the wisest thing that could be done; but I don't think it was delicate of them to come here at all. What do you suppose could have possessed them to do it, when they knew—"

"I don't believe they did know. It's something they couldn't realize; at least, Mevison couldn't. They've been fighting along for years, and as far as their nerves are concerned they're no nearer the end now than they ever were; their consciousness doesn't accept the fact. Mevison talked like a fool; I wanted to laugh. He would pitch into her, and pitch into himself, and then he would dwell on her good qualities, and he concluded, when we came off to bed, by refusing whiskey for his insomnia, because he was going to try some sleep-medicine that his wife had given him." Crombie ended in a note of hollow laughter which attested the derision in which he held Mevison's absurdity.

His laughter made his wife say "'Sh!" again, but she smiled herself before she added, severely, "Well, I hope they *will* separate. It will be the best thing for them. They can't respect each other after what they have done — or she has done. But what a dreadful thing to come into our lives!"

"I suppose we can stand it if they can," Crombie gloomily suggested. "I can't help being sorry for poor old Mevison."

"I am sorry for her, too. You can see that she's perfectly wrapped up in him."

"Well, she has a queer way of showing it."

"Not at all! But what I keep thinking of, all the time, is the effect it is going to have on Lillias."

"What has it got to do with Lillias?"

"It is such an awful warning."

"I hope it will be a warning to her to behave herself. She mustn't suppose that an Englishman will stand any such jinks as Mrs. Mevison's. It's a very good thing for Lillias."

"Perhaps. But oh, dear me! What a heart-breaking thing it is, Archibald, when

you come to think of it! We've never come
so near to a separation — other people's, I
mean — before. Isn't it strange that with
all the separating and divorcing that seems
to be going on, one has so very little of it
in one's own circle?"

"I'm not sure but there had better be
more of it."

"You know you don't think that, my
dear!"

"Well, anyway, I think I'll go to bed.
I'm awfully sleepy."

"Yes, you must be worn out by it. Good-
night, darling."

The epithet would not have seemed a very
close fit for Crombie with a dispassionate
witness, but these things are never intended
for the dispassionate witness, and perhaps
the kindly pair looked much the same in each
other's eyes as a younger couple might have
looked to one another.

Crombie might have been in bed half an

hour, and he had got distinctly past the border between drowsing and sleeping, when he heard a sort of scraping sound. He was aware of it scraping and scraping as if it were scraping through his sleep, and getting down to a dream beneath, and finally reaching the quick of his waking. He roused himself with a sense of having a head of balloon - like vastness and lightness, which, when he sat up in bed, seemed to sway and swing on his shoulders as if impatient for an ascent to the ceiling.

The instant he sat up, the gnawing or the scraping ceased. But he got out of bed, and went and bathed his eyes, so as to be ready for any emergency, in which quickness of vision was requisite, like that of a rat. The precaution aided in rousing him fully, and at once reduced the dimensions of his head, so that he had no difficulty in putting it out of the door into the hall and peering with his candle into its emptiness and silence.

Miss Bellard's Inspiration

It was so absolutely empty and so absolutely silent that the void seemed to mock his vision, and the stillness hummed in his ear with an audible derision. "Well," he said to himself, "I don't care what it was before, it isn't anything now. I probably dreamed it."

He went back into his room, however, and mechanically got into his clothes, and waited for that gnawing, or that scraping, to begin again. He was determined not to let it surprise him; he was determined to surprise it. With a resolution that affected him as adamantine, he drowsed again, and then started from his drowse, not to the accustomed noise, but to the sound, as he fancied, of a door in the hall quickly opened and quickly shut.

He flung his own door open, but again the innocent emptiness and silence of the dark hall offered themselves in a sort of gentle reproach of his turbulence. He waited, now,

a considerable time, but the emptiness and
silence maintained themselves in conscious
innocence, and after a vain prolongation of
his final scrutiny of the shadows he returned
to his chair.

This time he did not drowse; he could not,
he was so furious at being played upon—that
is, he did not believe he was drowsing, but it
was certainly not from a vigil that he again
started to his feet. Now he did not fling his
door open into the hall, but softly set it ajar
and waited on the threshold for the scraping
or the gnawing to begin. Then he was
aware of a soft movement in the hall, and a
figure, the figure of a woman fully dressed
and bearing a candle in one hand while the
other held her skirt behind from the floor,
as the fashion of women is, or lately was,
crept as with down-shod feet to the door of
Mevison's room and began to scrape on it
with her finger-nails. It was unmistakably
Mrs. Mevison, and, unless she was sleep-

walking, it was Mrs. Mevison inspired by a fell intent of which the conception almost bereft Crombie of his habitual politeness and the hospitable sense of the sacred character of a guest.

"What are you doing that for?" he whispered, hoarsely, harshly.

She turned and looked at him where he stood at his door, and measured him in mass and detail with an imperious eye. "I am trying to waken my husband," she answered, with a dignified calm which he could hope to emulate.

Crombie's belief was that she was doing it for pure mischief, and with a diabolical intent of tormenting her husband, who had probably locked the door between them to prevent her talking to him, but this was a belief which he could not well express even to a woman for whom he had tacitly allowed himself a wide range of disrespect. All he could do was to say, "Oh!" and stand

12

there till he heard a responsive stirring within Mevison's room.

After an interval long enough for Mevison to light a candle and get to the door it was unlocked and thrown open, and he appeared on the threshold.

"Oh, Arthur," she began, in the way people do who have been unexpectedly reminded, "I was just coming to tell you something I had thought of that will make us see everything in a new and different light; and—"

Her husband put his arm round her and looked over her shoulder at Crombie with a countenance of severe amaze. Then he murmured, "Come in, Clarice," and drew her inside the room and closed the door in Crombie's face.

The whole household slept late, and there was barely time for the Mevisons to get from the breakfast-table to the train that was to carry them to the Junction together. After what had happened at their last meeting, Crombie was not surprised that Mevison should bear himself somewhat awkwardly towards him. On the other hand, Mrs. Mevison was not only very sweet with Mrs. Crombie and Lillias, and tender with the waitress, to whom he afterwards saw her giving a tip out of all proportion to the length of her stay under his roof, but she behaved with extreme gentleness towards Crombie himself. He understood, as well as if she had put it in words, that this was in triumph over him and his suspicions; he surmised that she had been able to make Mevison make up their quarrel, and that between them they had offered him a sacrifice on the altar of their domestic happiness. As long as they were all together, Mevison did not relax from the stiffness with which he comported himself towards Crombie, but there came a moment when his wife did not keep the two men from meeting alone.

Mevison improved the chance, rather sheepishly. "My wife will tell Mrs. Crombie, but I think I ought to tell you, that Clarice and I are going to try it together again. She has seen our whole relation in a more possible light, and I must say that she has shown me where I have been in fault, and how I can avoid future causes of trouble. It's only right I should tell you that when you saw her last night she was impatient to tell me what she had thought of, and was trying to waken me without disturbing any one else."

"Oh, I understand that now, and I wish you would offer Mrs. Mevison my very sincere apologies for my seeming intrusion."

"I will, Crombie, with the greatest pleasure, for I know how glad she will be to feel that you are doing her justice. There is not a more generous creature under the sun."

"Oh, I can see that. I can see that it has been only her impulsiveness—I beg your pardon!"

"Not at all, old fellow. As I told you yesterday afternoon, though, I have been to blame myself. I see that more clearly than ever." They were both silent, for now they seemed to have come to the end of their say, but Mevison added, with an appeal as if from some profound insecurity, which Crombie found very affecting, "We feel as if we were beginning all over again, and I know that we are going forward on ground where there will be no room for the old—anxieties."

"I'm sure of that, Mevison."

"Thank you, Crombie—thank you!" Mevison's voice trembled a little, and he wrung his friend's hand hard.

Mrs. Mevison parted emotionally with all. She pressed Crombie's hand as if in recognition of a sacred confidence between them, and she exacted from Mrs. Crombie almost a promise that they would both come to see her when she and Arthur were settled in New York for the winter, though she knew how hard it would be for her to tear herself from her beloved Boston. She thanked Mrs. Crombie for having rescued them from that dreadful hotel, and she hoped they had not been too much trouble to her. She must let them pay her back for it somehow.

Lillias was the last to receive her adieux, and she told the girl she had purposely kept her for the last. "What shall I say to you, my dear?" she asked, from the sunny summit of her matronly felicity. "I wish you very, very happy, as the nice old phrase is. I wish you as happy as Arthur and I are going to be, for our honeymoon is just beginning over again. It seems a little selfish for us to be taking it before you have yours, but I suppose it can't be helped." She was clinging to the girl's hand, and fondly bending her eyes upon her from this slant of the head and from that, and now she humbly entreated, "May I kiss you?"

Lillias did not say, but perhaps she inclined her cheek a little. At any rate, she did not forbid the endearment, and Mrs. Mevison bestowed it.

"There!" she cried. "That's for good luck. Come, Arthur, dear! Good - bye, all! Oh! Why, Mr. Craybourne!" she called to the young man as he came round the corner of the house. "Just in time for hail and farewell!" She ran and seized his hand. "Goodbye! good-bye!" she cried, and she added in a stage whisper, for every one to hear, "Be good to that sweet girl!"

The carriage whirled her and Mevison away, but before it had traced the gravelled curve in front of the cottage Mrs. Crombie burst out with, "Treacherous, false, hypocritical, disagreeable woman!" in a diminuendo which seemed to do so little justice to the case that Crombie threw his arms desperately into the air and went in-doors without a word.

"I don't know," Lillias said, continuing to rub with her handkerchief at the cheek

173

which Mrs. Mevison had kissed, and staring after the carriage in a blank forgetfulness of Craybourne, who stood submissively by in expectation of her return to herself.

"*Lillias!*" her aunt cried.

"She's disagreeable, but you can't say she's insincere. She's shown out the worst that's in her, but can we be sure that *he* has?"

"Well, Lillias! After the rude way she behaved to you from the beginning!"

"I like to be just, Aunt Hester."

"Well, *I* can't make you out. Can you, Mr. Craybourne?"

Craybourne smiled. "Whenever I can't, I trust to a period of unconscious cerebration."

The girl looked at him with sudden wonder in her fine eyes and some apparent doubt.

"Well," Mrs. Crombie said, "I'm glad she's out of the house, anyway," and she added,

Miss Bellard's Inspiration

"What would you poor things like for luncheon?"

"Oh, anything, Aunt Hester. Or nothing." Lillias turned distractedly to Craybourne. "I want you, Edmund. Aunt Hester, excuse us a moment. I want to speak to Mr. Craybourne. No, no!" she said. "Don't go in! I'll take him down to the river. Come, Mr. Craybourne."

She left Mrs. Crombie looking after them as she led the way with Craybourne, swiftly swooping over the slope of the meadow, with her light skirt lifted before her and swirling in a fine eddy behind her.

She did not pause for the important talk which he felt impending till they reached that point of the river where they had sat the day before and thrown sticks into the stream and played the fool so gladly. Then she panted, "You see it won't do, Edmund."

He was not the sort of man to repeat her words in idle question; he sat silently down, and, with his kind, intelligent looks bent on her, let her go on.

"I am too much like her. I have been feeling it more and more; and unless you can prove to me that there is some vital difference, so that, under the same conditions, I should behave otherwise, it had better be off, and the sooner the better. I would rather be dead than treat you as she treated him, and *much* rather you would be dead than have you treat me as he treated her. I couldn't stand it for a moment, and I shouldn't respect you if you could."

Craybourne gave himself an interval of thoughtful silence before he asked, "Aren't you taking it rather too much for granted that you are like her? I don't see the least resemblance."

He had, certainly not with her connivance, but certainly not without her consent, possessed himself of that hand of hers which hung next him; and, now finding it in

Miss Bellard's Inspiration

his clasp, she pressed his hand gratefully. "I don't mean in temperament—"

"And I am sure not in temper!"

She pressed his hand again, and smiled sidelong up at him. Then as he folded himself down on the bank, she could not well keep standing, and, besides, she thought she could think better sitting. "I don't mean in temper, either; at least, I should hope not. But, Edmund, that has nothing to do with the kind of resemblance I had in mind. I am too much like her in being too much in love."

She looked anxiously at him, and as he had the instinct, rare among men, of knowing when not to laugh at a woman's seriousness, he did not even smile, and she went on:

"I should ask too much of you—"

"Ah, that," he broke in, "you could not do. You couldn't ask anything that I wouldn't gladly do."

"That is just what I should answer you,

if you had said what I said; and that convinces me that it is quite as bad as I supposed, if not worse. We are both too much in love."

He was as serious as she in replying, "Do you mean that people who are very much in love had better not marry?"

"That is what I mean. It is dangerous; it's madness to do so."

"I've sometimes vaguely felt it. But— Go on, Lillias."

She took her hand from him, observing, "If we kept that up, we never could talk sensibly, and I wish to talk sensibly."

"I'm afraid there's something in what you say," he sighed.

"Besides, this may be the beginning of the end, and we had better commence at once."

"What do you mean?"

"I haven't come to that, yet. But there is something—and it's the great thing, that I'm sure of—and that is that if we're marrying for love, we're making a mistake, and the more love the more mistake. We ought to marry dispassionately."

"I don't know that I should go so far as that," he said, with the fine reasonableness which she had early told him was his greatest charm. "But I certainly agree with you that love alone isn't a sufficient motive. I always supposed," he continued, with an introspective air, "that there was something besides love in our case. I thought there was a sense of character, an intellectual reciprocity, a mutual respect—"

"Yes," she said, "there's no denying that, and that's just what makes the love so dangerous. It's the mixture."

"Why," he argued, "you don't mean to say that there oughtn't to be *any* love?"

"No, I don't mean that, quite. It would be repulsive if there were *no* love. To marry for reason would be almost as bad as to marry for money."

179

Miss Bellard's Inspiration

"Then what do you think people ought to marry for?"

After a moment of sad reflection she said, "I'm not sure that they ought to marry at all."

"Lillias!"

"Of course, I don't mean that, either, quite. But after hearing what we've heard, and seeing what we've seen, all in a supposed union of hearts and hands that didn't admit anything of the kind to the world—"

"But why need we think that our marriage would be like that?"

"How do we know but all marriages are like that?"

"I'm sure they're not. There are your aunt and uncle: why shouldn't we be like them in our marriage?"

Lillias gave a fine, small shrug. "My aunt and uncle are ridiculous. Would you like to be like them? Darby and Joan are not my ideal."

"I don't think Darby and Joan are so bad when you get to their time of life. People come to Darby and Joan because they are good, I suppose, and kind to each other, and patient, and all that."

"Yes, but it may be the peace of exhaustion. They've simply fought to a finish."

"Well, my dear— Or perhaps you don't wish me to call you my dear?"

"You can call me so, provisionally."

"Thank you. Then, Lillias, I should like to know what you think was the attraction that brought us together, to begin with?"

"I don't know. Love, I suppose. At least, it was in my case."

"It wasn't in mine."

"It wasn't in yours!" She looked at him with the notion that he must be joking. But besides his being an Englishman, of whom joking could not always be predicated, especially on serious subjects, she saw that in this instance he was particularly in earnest. "I

should like to know what it was, then!" she
said, rather indignantly.

"It was interest in an experiment that had
my respect. It was what you were doing,
not what you were, that attracted me."

"Oh, indeed!"

"Yes."

"And may I ask what retained your interest?"

"It was you, your charming and adorable
self. But the sense of that certainly came
second and not first. Ah! I see I have
wounded you."

"Not at all. I like what you have told
me. It restores my self-respect. But it shows
me that men never can understand women.
When all is said and done, we are of different
natures."

Craybourne laughed joyfully. "Now that
is such an American way of putting it. So
delightful, so mystical!"

"And that is such an English way of

recognizing the fact. Yes, Mr. Craybourne," the girl said, getting unexpectedly to her feet, "we are not only of different natures, but different races."

"I always supposed the Americans and English were of the same race—the Anglo-Saxon race. Or if you won't allow that, we're certainly of the same human race."

"I'm not joking, Mr. Craybourne, as you seem to think. I see that we have never understood each other, and never can."

"I think we can. But why 'Mr. Craybourne,' Lillias?"

"Because I think it had better come to it at once."

"The—"

"Parting, yes."

He turned very white, very suddenly, so that she entreated, "Don't do that!"

"It isn't a thing I can help, quite. Lillias, why should we part?"

"You have the same as told me you don't love me—"

"No, dearest—or Miss Bellard, I mean—I said I didn't love you at first. And you had been saying that we oughtn't to love each other."

"Then you were deceiving me?"

He looked a magnanimous reproach at her unreasonableness, her unfairness, and she was ashamed. She took up a stitch she had dropped.

"I could see that all along you didn't care for me primarily as a woman. I piqued you and puzzled you as an American. I could see that you were always trying to make me out. And that was very offensive."

"I am sorry that I was offensive, but certainly you did pique and puzzle me, not only as a woman but as an American. Perhaps I piqued and puzzled you as an Englishman?"

"Not a bit. You were so much of a man that I could see through you instantly."

Miss Bellard's Inspiration

"I don't know what you mean by that."

"It doesn't matter. It's quite enough that we know our own minds at last. Our marriage would be unhappy because we are so hopelessly different, in nature, in nationality, in everything. I love you and I always shall—"

"And I you, Lillias, as long as I live."

"That is very sweet of you, Edmund. But we have had our lesson in those wretched people, and we had better heed it. You see yourself, dearest, that we could never remain united!"

"I don't see why we shouldn't try."

"Yes, dearest, you do. We can break now, and the cleavage would be absolute; but if we were married and broke there would be all sorts of picces. We have never had the least sign of a quarrel."

Craybourne was silent, perhaps absently, and she went on:

"And I determined from the first moment—"

"When was the first moment?"

"Why, I suppose it was the glimpse of you I caught that first day I saw you coming in to hear my lecture. I thought you were very distinguished, and I—well, I was taken with you. It began then."

"Did it, really? How intoxicating! I never knew that, Lillias."

"We've never talked out fully, yet."

"Then suppose we do it now."

"No, there isn't time, now. It's too late," she sighed.

"Oh, don't say that, dearest!"

"Yes, it's too late. According to what you say, you were not at all impressed so soon."

"Impressed?"

"Taken with me—it's the same thing."

"No," he owned, "I can't honestly say I was." Then he explained, "But I was taken with the idea of you, or what you were doing. I've always fancied women leading men in thought, you know; they're naturally our teachers. That sort of women were my heroines: Hypatia, and those two women who were university professors at Bologna, and the one at Padua; I don't remember their names; and when I heard, out there, that there was a woman lecturing to the students, of course I was taken—with the idca. I have always fancied intellectual women. I think they're peculiarly lovable. I dare say it's rather odd; a sort of taste for olives—"

Lillias remained gravely looking at him. Now, at the break in his continuity, she said, aloud, but as if to herself, "How ecstatically offensive!"

He stared blankly at her.

"Then I am—olives!" she explained.

"In the highest sense—well, yes."

"And I thought perhaps that I was roses, or violets, or lilies, poor fool!"

"Don't take it in that way, dearest! I supposed it would please you to know—"

"Please me!"

He gazed at her in a perplexity of such childlike simplicity that she could not help a very miserable laugh. "Really, Edmund," she said, as she turned and began to move homeward, "you beat the band. Now, don't," she added, angrily, "ask me just what I mean by beating the band. Any American idiot would know that."

She swept forward so swiftly that though he easily kept up with her, in his long, lank stride, his stride was quicker than usual. "Will you listen to me, Lillias?"

"No, I will not listen to you. I have heard too much already." She stopped as suddenly as she had started, and fixed him with scornful defiance. "I dare say that if we were married, and quarrelling, this is the point where you would call me a stubborn little fool."

"Oh, that abominable woman!" he groaned. "She has poisoned our love."

"Our love for olives?   Our peculiar passion for intellectual women?"

"You are cruel, Lillias, to take what I said in that way."

"You were cruel to say what I couldn't take in any other way."

"Then have patience with me for expressing myself badly!   For Heaven's sake don't let us quarrel!"

"Who is quarrelling?" she demanded.

"I mean, let us be reasonable.   You have always wished me to regard our affair dispassionately, and now you are giving way to a very mistaken feeling—"

"I am not giving way to any sort of feeling! You are worse and worse."

"Oh," he said, sadly, "I do seem to roil the water somehow, whether I stand up-stream from you or down."

"Poor lamb!" she retorted, contemptuously.   Then, after a few steps, she stopped again and challenged him: "And I am the wolf, I suppose!"

"Do you think it fair to accuse me of calling you a wolf?"

"You insinuate that I am unjust to you, when you know that I am the soul of justice!"

"I insinuate nothing, my dear. But I see that you are determined to break with me."

"Break with you? What is there left to break, I should like to know, after what has passed between us?"

"Very little, I'm afraid," he answered, with dignity. "And you are quite right. I accuse you of nothing; I take all the blame to myself for the beastly row that I should never have believed we would come to."

She stared at him, and the heat went out of her face, and a light of intelligence came into it, which was also consternation. "Yes, it *is* a beastly row, as you say, Edmund," she owned, with the frankness on which she prided herself. "It seems that we can't even part without quarrelling. Who would have dreamt it! And I meant that it should all be with such dignity, such self-respect, such consideration for each other! Oh, it isn't at all as I meant it to be! It's as bad as if we were married already. But you see, dearest, don't you, that we must part now? Doesn't it show you that we are not suited to each other? That I was perfectly right? Oh, dearest, how can you ever forgive me?"

She looked at him so tenderly, so ruefully, that he could not forbear giving her an object-lesson in forgiveness. The spot was secluded and convenient for the purpose, and he took her in his arms and laid her head on his breast, and she lingered for a moment in his embrace, as if gathering strength from it for the ordeal before her. Then she gently repulsed him and wiped from her eyes the tears which had accompanied her self-analysis from the point where it began to break in self-condemnation.

"Now," she said, "this is the end."

He seemed surprised at her announcement, as if he had supposed it were rather the beginning, but he had apparently not the courage to protest.

"We are parting," she continued, "not because we have quarrelled and are mad at each other, like two fractious children — though it nearly came to that—with me, at least; *you* are *always* divine—but because our reason is convinced that it is best; that we are not fit for each other, or at least I am not; and that if we married, we should go on squabbling to the bitter end. Oh, I am glad that it has turned out as it has, and that I have shown you what an unreasonable and impossible person I am, in time. So, good-bye, dear—"

"Don't you think," he inquired, very deferentially, "that it would be more, well, becoming, if I were to go back to the house with you, and—"

"Not for worlds! Why should you want to?"

"Merely for the effect with your family. I think it's due to them that I should say —that I should formalize our position, that I shouldn't seem to run away, or have been driven away—"

"I see what you mean, but I don't believe it's necessary, indeed I don't, dearest. If I did—"

"I went to your uncle when we first came here, and had it all out with him, and received his approval of my remaining, and now I think I ought to notify him of the conclusion we've come to."

"Yes, there's something in that. But Uncle Archibald wouldn't expect it. He wouldn't feel that it was due to him."

"I'm not sure that I don't feel it due to myself," Craybourne said, steadily. "I rather feel that it's my right not to have the appearance of skulking off."

"Oh, no one would dream of that! I can explain it to Uncle Archibald and to Aunt Hester both. You needn't be troubled. You may be sure that I won't let you suffer in their opinion. I shall take all the blame upon myself. But there *is* no blame! It's simply the wisest and best and kindest thing we could do for ourselves."

"Yes, I suppose it is—"

"Oh, it *is!* And now don't come a step farther! No!" The last word was accompanied by a swift evasion of the arms lifted towards her, and she fled away from him up the meadow and over the line where it began to be lawn. There she passed from his sight through a clump of shrubbery, behind which she hid, and watched him standing motionless, and then turning, and so walking slowly, head down, a pathetic figure, towards the ferry at the foot of the field.

XIII

ILLIAS went to her aunt as soon as she got to the house, and found her, with her spectacles on, doing some mending that would not admit the casual help of eye-glasses. "Aunt Hester," she said, sitting down without waiting to be asked, "Mr. Craybourne is not coming to lunch."

"Not coming to *lunch!* Why, I have got broilers, and strawberry short—"

"It doesn't matter. He probably couldn't eat a broiler as big as a grasshopper; at least, I couldn't. Or a single bite of strawberry short-cake. We have separated."

She had to endure having her aunt repeat, "Separated?"

"Yes, it's all off, and I propose being off

to-morrow morning. My week is up, and the Mellays will be quite ready to receive me. But if they weren't, I should go, anyway, somewhere, so that I could get away from this terrible place where I have been so happy." At this point Lillias put up her hands to her face to hide the peculiar expression she had noticed it always had when she was crying.

Mrs. Crombie had dropped her mending, and she now went on with an exclamatory, interrogative, objurgatory comment, until Lillias had got through crying and again took up her story.

"It's very nice of you to say that you can't believe it, and all that; and don't think I don't appreciate it. And it's very sweet of you to insist upon my staying, but my plans are made, and I shall go. And I'm not crying because I'm sorry that we've broken, but because we've broken in such a humiliating way."

"I don't see," her aunt ventured, "what you mean by humiliating, or what difference it makes *how* you break, so long as you break."

"It makes all the difference in the world when you have your ideal of breaking; and if you intend to do it with dignity, and carry conviction by reasoning it out, and the first thing you know you are trying to quarrel, it is humiliating. For the time being I felt just like Mrs. Mevison."

"I should have supposed," Mrs. Crombie said, very stupidly, as Lillias thought, "that if *she* occurred to you in any sort of way, it would have stopped you in your mad career."

"It was she that started me in my mad career. It was seeing what marriage could come to with no end of love, and—and—esteem, that gave me pause, and made me resolve to break with Edmund before it came to the sin and shame of such squabbling as went on with the Mevisons here. I reasoned it out perfectly, to myself, and I had just the expressions in my mind that would have left him without a word to say against it, when something he said before I could come to them started me off in another direction, and I was scolding and upbraiding him before I knew it, just like Mrs. Mevison. But, thank Heaven! *that* was convincing, anyway; and no matter what he thinks of my arguments, and considers me a wilful, capricious child, he must be glad he's well out of it. *I* certainly am. But what," Lillias demanded, with spirit, "makes you call it my *mad* career, Aunt Hester? Of course I know that you're my mother's sister, and all that, but I'm used to taking care of myself, and I don't think that as your guest I ought exactly to be called insane."

"I didn't mean that, Lillias. It was not the word I meant to use. I'm sure nobody could consider you more sane than I do. But—"

"But what? If you didn't mean insanity by mad career, what *do* you mean?"

"Why, I mean that you've thrown away a great chance."

"The chance to get married? I can get along perfectly well without being married. What great chance have I thrown away?"

"The chance of being married to such a man as Mr. Craybourne," Mrs. Crombie said, and she took back her mending into her lap again.

Lillias hesitated; perhaps she felt that there was reason in what her aunt suggested; but with a little spitefulness she asked, "What is so very remarkable about Mr. Craybourne, I should like to know?"

"Well, he is very unlike you, Lillias."

"Oh, thank you! Is that such a merit?"

Mrs. Crombie was on the track of a reason, and she was not to be put off the scent.

"He is an Englishman, and you would interest him as long as you lived. An American wouldn't be interested in you half so long. You would be just like a lot of other girls to him; like most of the other girls he had seen. But an Englishman is different. He has never seen any other girls like you— girls let loose, as it were—and he'd be always puzzling over you, and trying to make you out."

"Now, Aunt Hester, you have touched upon the very point that has been troubling me, and that I couldn't get at—like a pin somewhere. I don't think it's at all nice to have a man interested in you because you puzzle him; and in this case I don't think it would be fair to Edmund. I should be an imposition. But that isn't what I am getting at. Please go on."

The Old Woman in Mrs. Crombie felt somewhat baffled at the New Woman in Lillias, whom she vaguely suspected to be her spiritual as well as her intellectual superior; but in her belated way, she tried to go on. "He is not only an Englishman—whether you think it's an advantage or not to have your husband always interested in you; some girls would, I know—but he is a very good man. Any one can see that he's good by looking at him. I know he's rather romantic, but as long as he's romantic about you, I don't think that's any great fault."

"It is in a lover," Lillias interpolated.

"Then it isn't in a husband. They make the happiest kind of wives. I've seen it."

Lillias wondered if this meant her uncle, but she merely said, "Well, go on."

"And he is very intelligent. He is cultivated. He knows a great deal more than most American men. He's read more, and thought more. He isn't merely a business man."

"No, he certainly isn't a business man, poor fellow," Lillias noted, "or he wouldn't have made such a mess of his ranching."

Miss Bellard's Inspiration

"And no matter how high you went intellectually, he could follow you."

"Yes, he could even lead me; and our men, unless they make a profession of it, though they're bright enough, are not intellectual," Lillias reflected. "Well?"

"Well, that's all, I think. I suppose that once we should have considered whether he was religious or not; but the world has got to the pass where we don't consider that any more, when a man is good, and kind, and truthful, and fond of you. And so I say you have thrown a pearl away."

The girl was silent, passing her hand across her lap, and looking down at it in its passage. Then, "I know it, Aunt Hester," she said, "and it's just because he's a pearl that I've thrown him away—or it's as much that as anything. If he were less of a pearl I might have kept him."

"I can't make you out, Lillias."

"Why, it seems to me that I'm very clear.

Miss Bellard's Inspiration

We should have fought like cats and dogs, or Mevisons, not because he wanted to, but because I did. I should have made him do it, too. I couldn't have helped it. I'm so wrapped up in him, he's so all this world and the next to me that I couldn't have borne to have anybody else have the least look of him. I should have worried his life out of him. I saw it in time, and I stopped it. That's all. And the only regret I have is that I couldn't convince him of the fact without giving him an illustration. Well!" she rose with a quick sigh. "I suppose you will have to tell uncle?"

"Shouldn't you wish him to know? Don't you think it's his due?"

"Well, not perhaps till I get out of the house. I shall go the first train in the morning. Do you think you could keep it till then?"

"If you very much wish it," Mrs. Crombie said, with gravity bordering on offence.

"I do. And don't be vexed, Aunt Hester!"

"Oh no!"

"I think I should like to write to uncle about it. I believe he would understand. I'll write as quick as I get to the Mellays'. Could you wait till then?"

Mrs. Crombie promised. "Yes, I will wait till you can write to him."

"Thank you, Aunt Hester."

Mrs. Crombie looked after her as she left the room, not less baffled by her behavior about her uncle than by her behavior to her lover. Lillias immediately returned. "I don't think I shall stay with the Mellays long. I believe I shall go back almost immediately."

"Out there?"

"Yes. They wanted me to go on with my work, and now I should like to do so. It will be something to do. And I like it. I will write to the president, and when I hear from him I will go out there and begin preparing my lectures for the fall term."

"Well, you know what is best for you, Lillias."

"I used to think so," the girl said, sadly, and again she closed the door upon herself.

That afternoon, in default of anything else to say, Lillias having assigned a headache as her reason for not wishing to be provided for in any way, Crombie and his wife went on one of their drives. When they came back the girl could see by their looks of aggressive guiltlessness that her aunt had been telling her uncle everything. This was not unexpected to her, and Crombie was so openly embarrassed by the burden of the deceit imposed upon him, that she was fairly well amused by the spectacle, and she did not blame her aunt.

That night when Mrs. Crombie came in to help her with the last touches of her packing, or to offer help, she said, with a joyless laugh,

"We had better not have any concealments, Aunt Hester, and I won't pretend I don't know you've been telling uncle. I had no right to ask you not."

"Oh yes, you had," her aunt nobly protested. "And I really didn't expect to tell him. But I was so droopy that he noticed it, and then I had to tell him. We never keep anything from each other."

"No, and that is right. It is something I can never say of Edmund and myself, now."

"Oh yes, you can. That will all come right again. You are both so wise and sensible that I don't believe you'll let a little scare like those Mevisons spoil your lives."

"It's because we are so wise and sensible that we shall."

Lillias was leaning over her trunk with her hand stayed upon the lifted lid, and looking absently down at the freshly done-up shirt-waists in the top of it. Some sudden tears ran down her face and dropped on the shirt-waists. Her aunt rose from where she was sitting, and looked at the splotches on the shirt-waists.

"Never mind," she said. "If it leaves a blister, you can wait till you've had them washed."

XIV

THE next afternoon when Crombie was napping in his library (one of the uses of his library was to be napped in), he was roused by the titter of the electric door-bell, and the maid brought in Craybourne's card. Crombie was yet so dim with sleep that he looked at it for some time before he could say, with recognition, "Oh, send him in." He also called through the open door, "Come in, Craybourne." It had been such a relief to get the Mevisons out of the house, and then Lillias out of the house, that he had napped more deeply than usual, and it was not with a reasoned welcome that he hailed his visitor. As far as he could get himself aware of him, he realized that he thought he had gone, too,

Miss Bellard's Inspiration

and it was something like this he said when he stumped heavily forward and shook hands with the young man in appointing him a chair.

"No," Craybourne said, quietly, "I wished to see you before I went, and I didn't wish to come before Lillias had gone."

"You know she went this morning?"

"Yes, I saw her at the station."

It recurred to Crombie that Craybourne had seen Lillias at the station when she came, and his sense of the coincidence was embarrassed by the doubt he had always had whether Craybourne had not spoken to her on that occasion, and they both had decided not to recognize the fact in their very natural surprise at meeting afterwards under his roof. Partly this kept him from asking whether Craybourne had spoken to her on the present occasion, and partly the feeling that it would be indelicate. Craybourne helped him out by saying:

Miss Bellard's Inspiration

"I didn't speak with her, however."

"Oh," Crombie said.

"But I wished to speak with you, Mr. Crombie. I had a fancy it was your due, somehow, and at any rate the fact that I came here to talk with you about Lillias at first has controlled me so far that, well, here I am now. It may be the working of one of those odd subliminal—"

"Oh, don't get me on that kind of thing, my dear fellow," Crombie interrupted. "Smoke?" The young man shook his head, and Crombie said, "Ah, I remember," and lighted a pipe for himself. Then he remarked, as if it were a novelty, "Yes, she's gone," and sighed in a great whiff of nicotized expansion.

The young man took time, as if to let the fact sink in before he said, "When I came here first, a week ago—it seems much longer, and it seems no time at all; it's very strange! —I came to put myself frankly in your hands;

and if you bade me go away and not see Miss Bel—Lillias"—this new form of her name amused Crombie so that his mouth worked round the stem of his pipe in a smile which Craybourne was far too absorbed in himself to notice—"I was prepared to do so. Now I come prepared, if you say, to go after her."

"It's a free country," Crombie said, with a corner of his eye on the young man.

"I mean, if you think it's at all worth while. I don't pretend to be an American in these things, though I've taken out my first naturalization papers."

"One has to be more or less born to the case of a girl like Lillias," her uncle reflected for her lover's benefit.

"That is what I mean. You knew that we had broken, or rather that she had?"

Crombie thought it fit to say, "Mrs. Crombie mentioned something of the kind," not merely because it comported best with his own dignity to give it that casual turn, but because he felt that it politely reduced the fact to the insignificance it ought to have in Craybourne's eyes.

"Then the question is," the young man said, "whether, from the native American point of view, you not merely approve of my going after her, but whether you think it would be at all hopeful?"

Crombie got up for a match to relight his pipe, which he had been letting go out. "Do you mean to the Mellays'?"

"Has she gone to them? To be sure! I was thinking she had gone out there—"

"She's going, I believe, as soon as she's had her visit over with the Mellays. Excuse me, but how did you leave your affairs out there?"

"Oh, pretty much at sixes and sevens, I'm afraid."

"So that you would feel yourself justified in going out to look after them a little?"

"Entirely."

Crombie smoked a breath or two, nursing the knee he had taken between his hands in sitting down again. "It mightn't be a bad idea for you to be on the ground."

"On the ground?"

"When she gets there. I'm supposing you want it on again?"

"Decidedly, I want it on again!"

"Then it mightn't be a bad idea, and it might be a very bad idea. You'd have to take the chances."

The young man unfolded himself to his full height, as if about to take them on the instant. "Thank you, thank you—"

"Not at all. Though I don't mind saying that I shouldn't say this to everybody. But I think you're the man for Lillias, if there is one. I think you know how to take her, or *will* know. She has her ups and downs, and she's been looking after herself just long enough to suppose that she knows it all.

213

But she isn't a thundering fool, like that woman, Mrs. Mevison."

Craybourne smiled all over hope and joy. "She seemed to feel that we were somehow entangled in their fate because we were very much in love." He looked silly in taking the word on his lips, as a man always must before another man, as long as he is in love. "But I don't see how it follows. They quarrel because they are of the temperament for it, not because they are in love."

"There's a good deal of sense in that."

"It's what I urged Lillias to consider, but she seemed morbid, and couldn't bring her mind to it."

"You'll have to give her time. Perhaps she'll have brought her mind to it by the time you meet out there. Women think very quickly—when they do think. And they veer round like lightning."

"They're very strange," the young man said, blissfully.

" They're the devil and all for strangeness."

" But they're charming!"

" Some of them."

Craybourne put out his hand for good-bye and Crombie took it in getting up. " Going? I thought you might like to see Mrs. Crombie—"

" If it will do any good? Otherwise I don't think I'll disturb her, if you will make her my best compliments, and tell her how very kind I think she's been. But if you think I'd better see her—"

" No, on second thoughts, better not. She might queer it, and I confess that it won't stand queering, in my judgment. It's a very delicate situation. Let it be between us. I hope it 'll come out all right, but if it doesn't you mustn't blame me."

" No, certainly not. I—"

The stir of garments made itself heard, and Mrs. Crombie, who had been standing it as long as she could, up-stairs, after she knew

Craybourne was in the house, came in upon the two men. Her husband said to her casually, while she was greeting Craybourne, "Mr. Craybourne is going out there to wind up his business, and I've been advising him to wait till Lillias comes."

Mrs. Crombie seemed to have utterance, at first, for no more than a joyful "Oh!" though she made up for it afterwards, before Craybourne got away.

"Yes," Crombie said, proud of her approval, "I couldn't assure him that it would be all peaches and cream, but I think if they meet again on neutral ground there's a chance she may feel differently."

"Oh, I'm sure there is!" Mrs. Crombie breathed perfervidly. "Lillias is very reasonable. She was under the shadow of that terrible woman here, and she couldn't get away from the idea that she might somehow be like her; but I know she won't, and that she'll think so, too."

Miss Bellard's Inspiration

"It's very curious, isn't it?" Craybourne said. "It's a sort of obsession."

"Yes, indeed. All she has got to do is to forget her, and then she will see everything in its true light again. Lillias is very generous. She talked it over with me, and I know that she has no feeling against you; and that's the main thing."

"The other main thing," Crombie ventured a joke, "is that she still has a feeling *for* him. But that's what he's got to find out."

Craybourne would not let him have his laugh alone, but Mrs. Crombie remained grave, with her recurrent sense that Crombie was coarse, but her faith that he was always good even when he was coarse. "But Mr. Craybourne is coming to supper, isn't he?" she said, as if that were relevant.

"By supper," the young man answered, "I hope to be well started on my way. I shall take the five-o'clock train for Boston, and try to catch a Western train there. Or I can go by way of New York. I feel that everything depends upon my being out there somewhat before Lillias, so as not to have the appearance of following her."

"Yes, she wouldn't like that. But if you are there that will make all the difference."

"That is what I think," Craybourne said, and he and Mrs. Crombie went on talking it all over again, and leaving Crombie out more and more.

He was brought in again, after the young man had taken the leave he many times attempted, and Mrs. Crombie said to him, reproachfully, "Were you going to let him go, Archibald, without referring the matter to me?"

"Well, I didn't see the use of disturbing you. I thought you were lying down."

"And if it hadn't turned out well? I don't at all feel that it will. Where would you have been then?"

Miss Bellard's Inspiration

"Where I shall be now, if it doesn't turn out well, I suppose. I shall be responsible in any event."

"I don't see why you say that, my dear. Lillias is *my* niece, and I ought to have been consulted."

"Well, she's my niece, too, by marriage, just as much as you are my wife."

Mrs. Crombie looked baffled by his non-sense, as she finally looked grieved, but she left him, saying, there had been quarrelling enough in that house for one while, and that if he could laugh at such a serious matter she could not.

She forgave his offence, but it cannot be said that she entirely forgot it until she heard from Lillias, out there, a few days after her arrival. The girl wrote her aunt a very long letter and a sufficiently important letter, though Crombie professed to attach no special importance to it up to a certain point.

Her letter came at breakfast, and Mrs.

Miss Bellard's Inspiration

Crombie read it aloud, mumbling over the mechanical facts with which Lillias felt bound, as people do, to delay the appearance of the vital matters. Then Mrs. Crombie's voice grew more distinct, and her utterance more coherent. "'Of course,'" she read on, "'I could not honestly say that I was surprised to see him. I might as well confess, "right here," as the public speakers say in this section, that I should have been a little disappointed if I had not found him waiting for me, not exactly at the station, but somewhere on the municipal premises. His being here opened up the whole subject again, and when we had gone over it very thoroughly I could not see where the situation had changed in the least, and he was forced to acknowledge himself that it had not. The evening was ending—he came to call on me at the president's house, where they had asked me to stay till I could get settled— with our having decided neither of us ever

Miss Bellard's Inspiration

to marry, but both to remain friends, and see each other when we liked, without any silly consciousness, when he remembered something. He said he had forgotten to mention that Mrs. Mevison was staying at his hotel, and when I whooped at him, he said, Yes, he believed she had taken up her residence there in order to get a divorce. He had not spoken with her, but the young lawyer here who first told him about my lectures and brought him to hear me, has charge of her case, and he told Edmund.

"'Somehow, that seemed to throw a new light on the whole affair. I can't say just how it did, but it did. I sank down into one chair, and Edmund, who is only too glad to sink into chairs, so as to get rid of some of his ridiculous length, I suppose, sank into another. I instantly commanded him to tell me all about it, but it seems that he had told me at least all he knew, except the grounds for her divorce which her lawyer gave him.

221

"She alleges extreme cruelty and gross neglect of duty," Edmund said, and then we looked at each other, and though he has not the American sense of humor that we brag so about, even he could see the fun of this, and we burst out laughing in each other's faces. When I could get my breath, I said, "So they are going to separate, after all." "Yes," he said, and then before I knew it he was offering an argument that cleared me up to myself in the most wonderful way. I must try to give it to you in his own words, as nearly as I can, for I think it is very subtle, and does him great credit. He said, "Now you see, don't you, that this removes the only obstacle, the only real obstacle, in your mind?" I asked him if he meant that strange sort of feeling I had that we should be like them, if we married, and that there was not room in the world for two such quarrelsome couples, and he said that was just what he meant. "If they are separated

222

for good and all," he said, "don't you see that it gives us our chance? There is really no occasion for our breaking now, is there?"

"'Of course, there was a great deal more, and it was midnight before we had talked it all out; but midnight is nothing here, when a young man is calling. The point was a very fine one, and I kept losing it; but he never did; he has so much intellectual tenacity; and he held me to it, so that when he did go away, I promised him that I would think about it. I did think about it, and before morning I had a perfect inspiration. My inspiration was that where I was so helpless to reason it out for myself, I ought to leave it altogether to him, and that is why we are going to be married in the spring. We have agreed to wait till the spring term of the court is over, and see whether Mrs. Mevison gets her divorce or not. I know she will, but I am still a little morbid about it, and Edmund waits to gratify me. I shall enjoy giving my lectures during the winter, and he is going to look after his ranch, and see if he can get it into shape again, so that we can go out and live there.'"

There was more like this in the letter, but it was here that Mrs. Crombie broke off her reading to ask, "Did you ever hear of anything so absurd?"

"Absurd? No!" Crombie answered with robust decision. "I have had my moments of suspecting that Lillias was a fool, but this settles it. She has shown horse-sense."

"How can you be so coarse?" his wife murmured, fondly, with tears of entire satisfaction in her eyes. "She can make him go to England and live now, if she wants to. He will do anything for her. But you can see it wasn't a reason he gave her."

"Well, I suppose she didn't want a reason, if she had an inspiration."

THE END